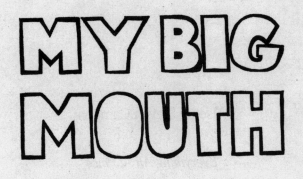

MY BIG MOUTH

Also by Steven Camden

Everything All At Once

Spoken Stories

MY BIG MOUTH

STEVEN CAMDEN

ILLUSTRATED BY CHANTÉ TIMOTHY

MACMILLAN CHILDREN'S BOOKS

First published 2021 by Macmillan Children's Books
an imprint of Pan Macmillan
The Smithson, 6 Briset Street, London EC1M 5NR
EU representative: Macmillan Publishers Ireland Limited,
Mallard Lodge, Lansdowne Village, Dublin 4
Associated companies throughout the world
www.panmacmillan.com

ISBN 978-1-5290-1097-8

1 3 5 7 9 8 6 4 2

A CIP catalogue record for this book is available from the British Library.

Printed and bound by CPI Group (UK) Ltd, Croydon CR0 4YY

For Dylan,
my cool and kind hero

chain reaction *(noun)*

A series of events, each caused by the previous one.

1

It all started when I was ten.

What was I like when I was ten?

Let me paint you a picture.

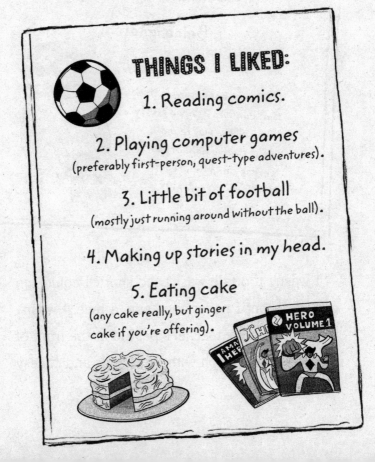

THINGS I LIKED:

1. Reading comics.

2. Playing computer games
(preferably first-person, quest-type adventures).

3. Little bit of football
(mostly just running around without the ball).

4. Making up stories in my head.

5. Eating cake
(any cake really, but ginger
cake if you're offering).

THINGS I DID NOT LIKE:

1. Custard (basically egg snot).

2. Those annoying people who just seem to be really good at pretty much everything without even trying.

3. Birthday cards with no money in. (What's that all about? 'Here you go, a slice of tree with some scribbles on it.' Whoopee.)

4. Being ignored.

5. Owls.

(I'm sorry, but any living thing that can turn its head pretty much all the way round whilst staring right at you is creepy, and those eyes? No thanks. Keep 'em.)

I wasn't too tall, wasn't too short. I could run quite fast, but I never once won a race. I wasn't the goody-goody teacher's pet kid at the front of the class photograph with jazz hands and cheesy grin, but I wasn't the tearaway rebel sneaking out of the shot to set the fire alarm off either. I was just in the middle. A regular ten-year-old boy.

And one thing I never was, ever . . .

. . . was cool.

2

I had a dog. Gus.

Same age as me.

Dad brought him home the week I was born. He said it was important to remember that human beings aren't the only species.

Lovable Gus. Rough fur like a toilet brush. He was a something crossed with a something else, like all the best characters, and nobody understood him like me. He slept in my room and I knew the sweet spot between his  shoulder blades that when you scratched it, made him roll over and howl a thank you.

Every now and then he'd get this crazy glint in his dark eyes.

Not crazy like *'I'm gonna bite your grandma!'*-type crazy. No. More like:

What's that?

It's your tail, Gus.

Nah, man. It's a snake.

Gus, it's your tail.

Snake.

Tail.

Snake!

Gus . . .

Snaaaaaaaaaake!!!!!!!!

That kind of crazy.

By the time I was ten, Gus was, like, seventy in dog years, which, looking back now, makes complete sense, seeing as all he did most days at that point was sleep underneath my bedroom radiator and fart.

But he was a great listener, and when everyone else would ignore me, I always knew I could count on Gus to share my problems.

OK, stop. Hold on.

Are you a dog person? That phrase means someone who likes dogs, but it always makes me picture a human with a dog's head.

If you had a dog's head, which dog would it be? I'd go with German shepherd, I reckon, or maybe one of those cool wolf-dogs with one blue eye and one brown eye. Yeah. Wolf-dog. Definitely.

Maybe you've got a dog? Have you?

Maybe as you read this, there's a dog curled up underneath *your* radiator, snoring a doggy snore and dropping the occasional fart.

Some people don't like dogs. The idea of a dog sleeping under their radiator is not one they enjoy. They're not dog people.

I am. I would happily have a dog in every room in the house.

I'm a cat person too. In fact, I'm pretty much an any-animal-in-the-whole-world person, really. Except owls.

You don't have to have a dog to be a dog person. Maybe you don't have a dog, but you'd like one. If you could have a dog, what would it look like? Would it be massive, or a tiny pocket dog that hides in your coat all day, yapping at strangers? Something in between?

What would you call it?

Say the name you chose out loud. Done? Good. Words are powerful. Ideas can come to life when you speak them. Trust me. It's like speaking them can make them real.

Speaking of names, what's yours?

Say it out loud. Nice. I could use that.

My name? Are you sure you need to know?

I could tell you that my name is Lord Dungfart

Trumplestink and it wouldn't matter whether I was telling the truth, would it? It wouldn't change what happened.

Exactly. But I suppose I should start honest, at least.

My name is Jason Gardner. People call me Jay. And I have a story to tell you.

We lived at number 184.

A skinny house in a street of skinny houses. Gus, me and three other humans.

HUMAN NUMBER 1: Mum

My mum was a nurse.

If you've ever met a nurse, or better still if you actually know a nurse personally, you'll know what I mean when I say that nurses are amazing. Doctors get all the glory when the news reporters do their interviews and they wipe their foreheads and strike a superhero pose after accidents, and they are pretty cool, but nurses, they're the ones who work the real magic day to day. It's a quieter magic that doesn't need to shout, but anything that's wrong

with you, a nurse can put it right, and my mum
was the super-mega-boss nurse.

Any time you felt bad, my mum knew what
to do to make you feel better.

Got a headache? Lie
on your left side in a
dark room.

Feeling a bit
sick? Peppermint tea
and a blanket.

Chopped your hand off? Grab some frozen
peas and a needle and thread.

Anything at all that broke, Mum could fix it.

Thing is, though, nurses work crazy hours.
Mum would sometimes work all night and sleep
during the day. When she was working nights,
we had to tiptoe around the house so as not to
wake her, because trust me, you do not want to
face Mum if you've
woken her up mid-
sleep. She used to
wear these:

You've seen these before, right? On aeroplanes if you've ever flown on one. Or in old films. You don't see them much in regular life because, to be honest, I'm not sure they actually work. Mum's definitely didn't. I'd come home from school, tiptoe in, step on one creaky floorboard, and Mum would come downstairs making a face like someone who'd just sat on a porcupine.

She loves music. Favourite type of music? Reggae. I'm assuming you've heard of Bob Marley? Reggae legend and cultural icon? If you haven't, don't worry, just go and make use of the internet and listen to his music and then come back. He's amazing. Mum's ultimate favourite. She used to sing 'Buffalo Soldier' when she was cooking. She doesn't have the greatest voice, but she always went for it full passion, you know?

I'd be sitting on my bed, reading a comic, Gus fast asleep under the radiator, and the smell of dinner would come wafting up the stairs as Mum's amateur-reggae-star voice boomed through the floorboards.

HUMAN NUMBER 2: Donna

My older sister.

Four and a half years older than me. If you've got an older sister, you'll understand how special and complicated they can be.

If you don't, let me explain something: older sisters are STRONG. Older brothers might make more noise, but in a one-on-one situation, I'd take an older sister every time. Maybe I'm biased because my older sister Donna was a fourth-dan black belt in kung fu. You ever heard of Bruce Lee? Martial arts legend? Movie star and cultural icon? If you haven't, don't worry, just go make use of the internet, find some old clips and then come back. He's amazing. Donna's ultimate hero.

Donna was that girl at school who nobody messed with, not even boys. Everybody knew that if you started something with Donna, it usually ended up with you on the floor holding your bruised neck.

The thing about an older sister is (and if you have one, you'll know this), she is either your best friend, or your worst enemy. It depends on the day.

On some days, she's amazing. Like the time I came off my bike and cut my knee open, and Mum wasn't around. Donna cleaned it up, put me on the sofa, wrapped my knee in a bandage, gave me a blanket and a sandwich and the remote control. Perfect.

Then there were other days, when she used to just roll me up in my own duvet, and sit on me. All afternoon.

Punching me every time I squirmed and forcing me to call her 'master'.

If your older sister is old enough to be going out on dates, here's a tip I learned the hard way. You never EVER mention her love life, and you never EVER EVER tell your older sister that you think she looks good. Something about a compliment from their little brother is basically older-sister kryptonite. One time last summer, Donna came downstairs after dinner in her best dungarees and jean shirt, and I foolishly said something like, '*Oh, Donna, you look lovely. Who's the special person?*' And . . .

CHOP! – straight in my neck – then she stormed off to her room and blasted her music while she got changed, leaving me in a crumpled heap on the hallway floor.

Donna's music isn't reggae like Mum's. Donna's music is all made by bands full of boys with hair across their faces who play guitar and wear ripped clothes and sing songs about how everything's rubbish and nothing really matters and we're all just going to get old and die.

So there were times when I'd be sitting in my room, with Donna's moody music blaring through the wall, the boom of Mum's reggae voice coming through the floor, and me and Gus just stuck in the middle like some kind of musical sandwich.

HUMAN NUMBER 3: Dad

My dad was a funny one.

Kind of up and down. On good days, he was amazing.

He used to make up stories. That was his job. Writer. He wrote books for grown-ups that I wasn't allowed to read, but I didn't really care because the stories he made up on the spot for us were so good. Best stories ever. Stories about getting sucked down the bath plughole to fight ninjas in the sewer. Stories about jumping out of bed in the morning and realizing you've turned into a rhino from the waist down. Incredible stories.

When he told them, it felt like he pulled you in with him and you were almost living a movie inside your own head, directed by the coolest person alive. So much fun.

Me and Donna used to sit on the living-room floor looking up at him as he spoke, feeling like we were witnessing actual magic. Then, when Donna got older and it was just me sitting there, Dad would let me help create characters and even sometimes do the voices. He used to say that stories are what bring us together.

I remember on my seventh birthday, he pinned a laminated map of the world up on to my bedroom wall, one of those massive ones, that covered the entire space between my door and the window, and on the nights when he wasn't working, before I went to sleep, Dad would sit on the edge of my bed and ask me to point to a place on the map. I'd stick out my finger at some random location, and Dad would then make up a story about that place. Greenland. Fiji. Cameroon. Out of nothing. Just like that. So cool.

I remember asking him once, I was like, 'Dad, aren't you just lying?'

Dad looked right at me and said:

'No, Jason. See, there's a difference. A lie is selfish. And a story is a gift. You'll learn.'

Coolest stories ever.

On the good days.

On the bad days, it was best just to leave him alone. Either in his room, at the desk, or downstairs in his chair. See, my dad had a chair. If your dad has a chair, then you'll know the unspoken rule:

WARNING:
NOBODY SITS IN DAD'S CHAIR!

Like he's the king and the chair is his throne or something. I'm not sure why mums don't seem to get chairs. They're the ones who do most of the real work, as far as I can see, but none of them ever seem to demand their own chair like dads do. I don't know who made that rule up or if it's carved on the inside of some cave wall somewhere, but my dad had a chair and only he sat in it.

Something I noticed from when I was really

small was that people always seemed fascinated with what dads did. Like what your dad did for a job was some super-important information. Like if your dad had a cool job it somehow made you cool. I'm not sure who decided what jobs are cool and whether there's some list written somewhere with all the cool jobs on, but people always wanted to know. You could have said anything. Just kept a straight face.

What does your dad do?

My dad is . . . an astronaut.

Really?

Yeah.

My dad is . . . a professional wrestler.

Really?

Yeah.

My dad is . . . an international assassin.

Really?

Yeah.

My dad . . .

. . . disappeared on a Sunday night while we were all asleep.

4

It was the start of summer half-term in Year 6.

A whole week off before the last five weeks of my junior school life. I woke up, ready for a fun-filled week of computer games and cartoons. And he was gone.

Like someone had come along with some giant scissors and cut him out of the family photograph.

He left hardly anything behind.

A few old clothes.

A shelf full of his old mystery novels and reference books.

A pair of worn-out shoes.

His flat cap.

And his toothbrush.

Was he coming back? Where had he gone? Why did he leave?

These were the questions swimming round my brain, but whenever I tried to ask, Mum or Donna would change the subject.

We don't think so, they said.

Not now, they said.

It's complicated, they said.

Short, snappy answers, with pretty much no information in them, the whole time their faces letting me know they thought I was too young to understand. It felt like our house was holding its breath and I didn't get how they could just carry on, doing normal daily stuff. But that's what they did, and it seemed like that's what I had to do too.

The weirdest part of when someone leaves is the space. The normal places where you used to see them being empty. The bathroom. By the fridge. Their chair.

It's not like when someone is just out, at work or visiting friends. When someone leaves, the spaces you used to see them in almost feel like they've changed colour. Like a T-shirt that's gone through the washing machine twenty times. Kind of faded.

I don't know if that even makes sense, but it's what I mean.

After a couple of days, Mum gathered up all of Dad's old stuff into a bin bag and took it to the charity shop. The last bits of evidence that he lived here vanished just like him. But she forgot his toothbrush. Maybe she didn't notice it. Maybe she wasn't sure it was his, but it stayed there, in the little yellow plastic cup next to the bathroom sink.

Every morning and night, that whole week of half-term, I had to look at it as I brushed my teeth. And every time I looked at it, I felt myself filling up with questions.

Mum kept putting on a smile and saying I was now 'the man of the place', and even though that did feel kind of cool to hear, I still wasn't getting any answers.

Honestly, if it hadn't been for Gus, I think I would have gone completely mad that week. Sitting on my bedroom floor in my pyjamas each night, looking out at the silver hook of the moon, I shared my thoughts and questions with Gus, and, even though he didn't have any answers, just like always, Gus listening calmed me down.

A whole week of brushing my teeth every night and every morning, staring at his toothbrush sitting smugly in the cup. Like even it knew more than me.

Then, on Monday morning, first day back for the last five weeks of Year 6, I snapped.

Brushing my teeth that morning, staring at his toothbrush, I could feel myself pressing too hard, the bristles of my brush scratching at my gums as the toothpaste froth spilt out on to my chin. I felt the word coming out of my mouth: 'Enough!'

And a switch inside me flipped.

I spat, grabbed Dad's toothbrush from the cup, threw it into the toilet and flushed.

That'd show him.

If I didn't get any proper answers to my questions, then he didn't get to leave his toothbrush there and make me think about him every single morning and night. I'd flush him away.

Gone.

It didn't flush.

I tried again.

And again.

I tried seven times. Have you ever tried to flush a toothbrush down the toilet? If you have, you'll know. It doesn't work. Something to do with a lack of density or something.

In the end I had to pick it out with my fingers like tweezers, and throw it into the bin.

Not as dramatic, but I'd done something. Something that mattered. The air in the house felt different. Like I'd popped a balloon. And I felt a kind of ticking in my stomach, like something had started.

And that was because it had.

Are you familiar with the term 'chain reaction'?

One thing happens, which causes something else to happen which is a bit bigger, which causes something else to happen which is a bit bigger, which causes something else to happen which is a bit bigger, and before you know it, you're trapped under a big mess that you can't control. Well, on Monday morning, first day back for the last half-term of Year 6, I started a chain reaction, with a toothbrush.

5

Walking into school that morning I met Dominic outside Mr Rogers's corner shop like always.

DOMINIC

Dominic Clarke. My best friend. Best friend since nursery.

Have you got a friend you've had since nursery? If you do, and you're still close to them, you'll know that it means you're basically family. We'd do sleepovers at each other's houses. His mum knew my mum and his older brother Noah was in the year above Donna at secondary school.

We were both two of the youngest in our year. His birthday was just before the end of school and mine was in the summer holidays, which

29

meant by the time we were ten, a lot of our class were nearly eleven.

Dominic was about the same size and shape as me, but he had light skin and fair hair and every summer he suddenly got freckly, like someone had snuck into his room while he was sleeping and dotted his face with a copper felt tip. Dom had this crooked smile that made it look like even when he was happy, he was still slightly confused.

We were into most of the same things: we shared computer games, swapped comics and had the same calculator watch – you get the idea.

One thing that was different about us, though, was that Dominic was into big gestures.

He loved doing dramatic things. Like the time he made himself a flying-squirrel costume out of his dad's overalls and was going to jump off their garage to test it. Luckily he had called me over to be his witness, and I managed to tease him down from the garage roof with fizzy laces and questions about black holes, before he splatted himself on their driveway.

Dominic loved science, especially outer space. If you got him started on the Big Bang, you better grab some popcorn and a comfy seat because he could (and often did) go on for hours.

The best thing, though, when I think on it now, was that he wasn't fussed about what people thought. Dominic just concentrated on the things that he liked and what made him happy. He never bothered about what other people thought was cool. I used to say I didn't care, but deep down I did. I always wished I was cool.

He used to eat fish-paste sandwiches.

Have you ever had a fish-paste sandwich? If you have, you know.

If you haven't, picture a bowl of fish in your lap. Got it? Big bowl of fish, happily swimming around, la-di-da. Now grab a wooden spoon, and mush them up – mush mush mush – and keep on mushing them up until all you're left with is a brown sticky paste that stinks like fish. Now spread that on some floppy white bread, and bingo. Fish-paste sandwich. Want one? Me neither.

Dominic did. He ate them almost every day, and even when people would point and shout, 'Eurgh! You're disgusting, you're eating poo sandwiches!' Dominic would just smile with his mouth full and say, 'Yep. I'm eating poo. Mmmm.'

He really didn't care like I would have. Kind of amazing.

When I met him that Monday morning, he'd been away with his family for half-term and I hadn't spoken to him for the whole week so when he showed up with a buzz cut I was so shocked I almost forgot about Dad.

'What the hell, Dom?'

Dominic just shrugged. 'Yeah. Noah was supposed to give me a trim, but then he "slipped" and here we are. At least it'll improve my aerodynamics.'

As we walked to school he broke down his trip to the caravan park. How he'd spent the whole time befriending one particular seagull with breadcrumbs, with the intention of training it to go on missions for him and be his 'eyes in the sky'.

'How did you even know it was the same bird?' I said.

Dom just rolled his eyes. 'Distinguishing marks, Jay. I'm not stupid.'

I wanted to tell him about Dad. But at the same time I didn't want to. I wanted to share my messed-up half-term news, but I didn't know what to say. It felt weird and the truth is, I was embarrassed. Like I'd failed at something. Like I'd done something wrong.

'You OK, Jay?' Dom asked as we approached our school. I could hear squeals from behind the playground wall.

'I flushed my dad's toothbrush down the toilet.'

'What?'

'Doesn't matter.'

'Why?'

A car beeped its horn and we both jumped. We both stood still outside the gates. I could feel my face getting hot as I looked at Dom.

'It didn't work. It wouldn't flush. So I threw it in the bin.'

I walked into the playground. Dom followed me, his face covered in what looked like concern.

'But. How will he brush his teeth?'

I shrugged.

And then we saw the poster.

Hold on a second.

Have you ever had something you wanted to tell

34

someone, but then when the time came for you to tell them, it somehow didn't feel right, so you didn't, and then the moment felt like it had passed by like a train you were supposed to be on?

I didn't tell my best friend about Dad leaving that morning. Why?

I could say it was because I couldn't think of the right words. I could say it was because I didn't think he'd understand, but the truth is, I think it was because I didn't understand myself.

Dom stood staring at the poster, which was big enough to almost cover the glass doors to reception. In among the stars and glitter were the words:

TALENT SHOW!

END-OF-YEAR TALENT
☆ COMPETITION! ☆

BE A
WINNER

It didn't mean anything to me, but I watched Dom's face light up like Fireworks Night.

'Yo. We're gonna win!' he said.

I could already see familiar figures scattered around the playground. A few people were playing football. Marcia Brown & Lucy Cheung were dancing over a skipping rope while a semicircle of other girls gave them a round of applause. Dominic punched my arm.

'Do you hear me?'

'Ow. What?'

He pointed at the poster. 'Me and you, talent-show winners, school legends!'

He had the same crazy look in his eye as Gus gets.

'What are you talking about?' I said, rubbing my arm.

Dominic balled his fists and pressed them against his temples. It was what he did when he was trying to think.

'School legends, man. Me and you!'

'Don't be stupid, Dom. What exactly would we

do, eh? What possible thing could me and you do to win a talent show?'

Dominic lowered his hands. 'I dunno yet. But it's gonna be awesome.'

Then the bell went.

As we walked inside, I could see from the look on his face he wasn't going to think about anything else for ages, but I was still thinking about Dad's toothbrush and the ticking feeling in my stomach, and as we sat down in class and Mr Bukowski started to take the register, I just knew something was coming.

6

Have you got a favourite teacher?

I think even if it's just the one who annoys you the least, there's probably a name you could say. Something about human beings makes us choose a favourite.

OK, so think of your favourite teacher. Now try and think what they might be doing right now. Picture your teacher somewhere normal. At home, making a cup of tea. Standing in front of the cereal in the supermarket trying to choose between loops and flakes, or in the shower, singing some ancient pop song while they scrub their back. Go on. Try.

It's hard, right?

Thinking of any teacher anywhere outside of school is weird. It's just the way it's always been. It's like trying to picture Santa naked.

I definitely had a favourite teacher though.
His name?

MR BUKOWSKI

Picture a badger. No. Wait. Forget the badger.
Picture a bear.

Take a second. Any bear. Polar. Grizzly. Pizzly.
Doesn't matter.

You got it? Close your eyes if it helps. Now
zoom in on just the bear's head. On the face.
Yeah? With me? Got the bear's face? Right.

Now shave it.

Shave off the fur, but leave a little beard, and
tufts above both ears. Done it?

Now put glasses on him. Those round glasses
that make anybody look clever. Yeah?

Right, now give him a smile. A warm, friendly-
bear smile. Got him?

Bingo. Friendly shaven bear. Mr Bukowski.

He loved stories. I loved stories. We got along.

He had one of those calm voices. You know

the ones? Like, super-silky calm.

I mean, super-silky, golden-sticky-honey stupidly calm. The kind of voice that could stop water boiling. Say the following sentence out loud in the calmest voice you can:

'Good morning, everyone. How was your weekend?'

Try it again. Calmer.

Now imagine a voice twenty-seven times calmer than that, and you might be halfway there.

Mr Bukowski's voice was like the sound of a

blue whale's heartbeat, which is about ten times slower than your heartbeat.

If you were on a plane, and it was going to crash into the sea, you'd want Mr Bukowski sitting next to you.

You: 'AAAAAAAAHHHHH! We're gonna diiiiiiieeeeeeeee!!!!!'

Mr Bukowski: 'Don't worry. Relax. Breathe. Yes we're going to crash, but if you think about it, the ocean is a truly fascinating place full of wonderful creatures, we're actually very lucky. Mmmmmmm.'

That kind of calm.

In fact his voice was so calm, that if he ever got even slightly angry for just one single split second, it was like the switch was too much for your brain to handle and you completely froze. Which is exactly what I did, that Monday morning, when he called me out to the front of the class.

Book reports.

You've done one before, I'm sure. If you haven't, lucky you. There aren't many things that will squash your enjoyment of something more than having to write a report on it. The routine went:

1. Choose a book.

2. Take that book home.

3. Read it.

4. Write a page-long report on it.

5. Bring it back to class.

6. Stand up in front of the class and deliver your report to everyone.

Dominic loved them.

He always managed to find a book somehow related to space, and prepared detailed presentations about Jupiter's orbit or whatever.

I hated them. Public speaking was not my thing at all.

I'd grabbed some random book on Friday afternoon when we broke up.

My plan, as always, was to leave it until the very last minute, and then get it done the night before school started again, in a state of combined panic and frustration. But I didn't. Because of Dad. And not getting answers. And his toothbrush. All of it.

To be honest, I don't even remember the title of that book now but, whatever it was, I hadn't even picked it up, let alone opened it and read it. I hadn't even thought about writing a report. And now, there I was, standing in front of the entire class, feeling like I was naked on stage as everyone's eyes burned into me, waiting for me to speak.

'We're waiting,' said Mr Bukowski in his stupidly silky calm voice.

I scanned the room. The familiar cast of classroom characters now felt like a blood-hungry mob of Roman citizens at the Colosseum, waiting for my sacrifice. Dominic was pretending to scratch his face, giving me the sneaky thumbs up, thinking he was helping.

Trying to avoid him, I looked towards the back left of the room. And that's when I saw him.

DANNY JONES

Most of us know a Danny Jones.

They might not share the same name, but they're pretty similar characters in all our stories, and that character is . . .

THE BAD GUY

Danny Jones was in the same school year as us, but he looked, like, five years older.

45

He walked like he was trying to crush paving stones with each step, swinging big boulder shoulders that were genetically designed for pushing you over.

His older brother was known locally as an actual gangster and the whole family had these kind of puffed-out chunky cheeks like some kind of hardcore hamsters.

Danny was captain of the football team and the fastest in PE. Everyone always laughed at his jokes, even though they were never really any good, and if he gave a wrong answer to a question in class, nobody ever laughed behind their hands. That guy.

For some reason, he didn't like me. I never really understood why, but I think that's just the way it works with bullies.

One time, he tied me to the tree at the back of the playground with my own jumper and practised taking penalties, shooting at my face. I don't know if you've ever had a football booted straight into your face before, but if you have, you'll understand the level of torture. When Dominic tried to stand up to him and help me, Danny tied Dom up too, and the pair of us had to wait for the whole of lunchtime to pass until the bell went and the dinner lady finally saw us and came to the rescue.

That's Danny Jones.

And now he was staring right at me. Like only he could. The kind of stare that could burn a hole into wood. Like any second he could just jump up, grab me and eat me.

Like chewing me up and spitting out my bones would be easy.

I felt like I was going to melt. Or pass out. Or pass out, then melt. A puddle of me on the classroom floor.

'We're still waiting.' Mr Bukowski's calm voice.

Danny Jones's stare.

Crazy Dominic over there.

Marcia Brown & Lucy Cheung were starting to giggle, then I felt the ticking in my stomach again. Like a clock in my belly. But this time it was moving. Up. Inside my chest. Up. Along my throat. Up. And I opened my mouth and . . .

lie *(noun)*
A false statement made with deliberate intent
to deceive; an intentional untruth; a falsehood.

FOR MAXIMUM EFFECT, READ THIS NEXT BIT OUT LOUD. START AT YOUR NORMAL SPEAKING PACE, THEN, EVERY TIME YOU SEE A ✽, GET **FASTER**, UNTIL YOU'RE LITERALLY SPEAKING AS FAST AS YOU CAN AND MIGHT FALL OVER. IF YOU'RE IN PUBLIC, EVEN BETTER. THREE...TWO...ONE...**GO!**

'I'm sorry, sir. I haven't done it. I haven't done the book report. I didn't have time. I mean. I was too busy. Helping my dad. ✽ Yeah. I was, helping my dad. With his new story. See, that's what he does, my dad. He writes stories. ✽ His new story is all about a secret agent, travelling the world doing different missions, so that's what he's doing. My dad. ✽ He's pretending to be a secret agent, travelling the world. For research. And I'm helping him. It's pretty full on. See, what he does is, he phones me up from wherever he is and tells me to choose a place, and then I look at the map, choose a place and that's where he goes to next. ✽ It's to keep people guessing. It's top secret. The publishers are paying for it, sir. I have to research the places he's going to so he has all the details he needs. And with time zones and everything. ✽ On Sunday night he called from Sydney, Australia, sir. They're twelve hours ahead. Dad said it's so hot there, you can fry an egg on the bonnet of a car. ✽ I had to wait up, and tell him facts that I'd researched. I hardly slept at all. I meant to do the report yesterday, I swear, but then Dad. And the mission. I'm sorry, sir. ✽ I haven't done the book report, but when your dad calls and asks for help on a secret writing mission, you can't say no, can you?'

NOW **BREATHE**. IF YOU DID IT RIGHT, YOU SHOULD BE ABLE TO FEEL YOUR LUNGS INSIDE YOUR CHEST, AND YOUR SKIN SHOULD BE TINGLING LIKE A MILLION TINY PINS ARE MARCHING OVER YOU. **JUST LIKE MINE WAS**.

It felt like something had exploded deep inside me. Something strong that I couldn't explain. Waves of energy radiating out from my stomach, filling me up. A force.

I just stood there like a glowing nuclear statue of myself, looking at my class. Every one of them was still staring, but it felt different. Like they'd all just got camera-flashed by a lighthouse-sized bulb.

Danny Jones's face looked like he was trying to do long division inside his head.

Marcia Brown & Lucy Cheung were staring at me with tilted heads like I'd just pulled my own face off like a mask or something.

'Thank you very much, Jason,' said Mr Bukowski, and I noticed the tiniest ripple in the calm of his voice. 'You can sit back down,' he said, smiling.

So I did.

I went back to my chair, my skin still tingling, and sat down.

Dominic's eyes were wider than dinner plates, and as Mr Bukowski started the lesson, and the rest of the class snapped back to life, Dom leaned over and whispered, 'Yo! Why didn't you tell me?'

'Tell you what?' I said.

'About your dad's new story. The mission!' His face was completely serious.

I felt my own face screwing up. 'Dom, it's not true, is it?'

Dominic looked at me like I was making no sense at all. 'Which bit?'

And it hit me. My best friend believed me. The stream of words that came from somewhere inside me and out of my mouth in the moment. My dad? On a secret writing mission? How was that even possibly believable?

I didn't know. But it was. I made it up, and

Dominic believed me. Seemed like the rest of the class believed me too and, strange as it sounds, in that moment, I almost believed it myself.

I took a deep breath and the air felt different.

I just sat there, breathing it in, and the best word I can think of to describe how I felt, right then, is . . .

. . . powerful.

***

####### **TIME OUT** *******

See.

The thing about books is, well, it's just reading, isn't it?

Don't get me wrong, I love reading. I would say now that reading is probably one of my top eleven things to do, but just like anything else, too much of one thing, in one go, it's just, well, it's just dry, isn't it?

You've met a lot of people already and if you're

anything like me, it's hard to remember names. Danny and Dom both start with the same letter which is extra-confusing too.

Dom: Good guy.

Danny: Bad guy.

Try saying everyone's name you can remember out loud that we've met so far.

Yeah? How many?

OK. Pretty good. Now I suggest you take a break.

Get a biscuit. Stroke your dog if you have one. Tickle your little brother or sister if you have one of those. Do some yoga. Have a power nap. Then come back.

Do it. I'm serious.

We have a lot to get through.

Done?

Ready?

All right, then. Let's get back to the story.

Sitting by myself in the busy hall that Monday lunchtime eating my apple, I could feel people staring. Hear them whispering.

'Psst. Yo. Yo. That's him. The kid . . . What kid? . . . With the dad. His dad. And the story. The mission . . . What mission? . . . The secret mission!'

Now, you might think it'd feel weird. Sitting there, eating your apple, everybody watching you, muttering to themselves, but it didn't. It felt great. Like I said, I felt a power. And something else. Sitting there, eating my apple, all eyes on me, I felt something I'd never felt before.

I felt cool.

Then Dominic crashed into the seat opposite me, out of breath, carrying a small stack of printer paper.

'Where've you been?' I said, still feeling like I was on stage as I spoke.

Dominic just gasped for breath and slid a piece of paper across the table that had this on it:

'What's this?' I said, holding the paper.

Dominic stared right at me, fire in his eyes and said, 'That's us!'

'What?'

'Me and you,' he said, making a fist in the air between us. 'Full Force!'

I looked at the wobbly picture, then back at him. 'What?'

Dom grinned. 'Talent-show winners. School

legends. Me and you. Full Force!'

'What's full force?'

'Me and you! Are you listening? Talent-show winners! I've put them up all over school. We've got to create a buzz. We're gonna win! Full Force!'

Every time he said the words, his fist shook like it was about to explode.

'What the heck is Full Force?' I said.

Dom smiled his crooked smile.

Stop.

Right there. Look at the picture.

If he'd slid a piece of paper with that wobbly drawing and those words on it to you, what would you think it meant? Any ideas? What was Dominic's big idea for me and him to win the end-of-year talent show? It's not obvious, is it?

I'll tell you.

Dancing.

Yep.

Dancing.

Now, if you knew Dominic Clarke as well as I do, your face would be screwed up like a confused squirrel sucking a lemon.

Dominic Clarke can't dance. At all.

I'm sorry, he's my oldest friend, and it's not like I'm the greatest mover myself, but at least I can hold a rhythm. Dominic, though, is fully awful.

Think of the worst dancer you know. Your crazy uncle who has too much to drink at New Year's. Your mum or your dad with their weird parent two-step zombie shuffle at a birthday party. Whoever you're thinking of, Dominic was worse. Way worse.

Let me give an example.

Christmas holidays, Year 5. We went to his Aunt Sheila's wedding.

He brought me along for the cake.

Now, you know that part of a wedding after all the boring promises and the kissing, when everyone watches the new bride and groom share the first dance, and claps and cries, then the DJ shouts, 'OK, everybody on the dance floor!' and everyone rushes on to cut some rug, and it's a big party, right?

Well, at Aunt Sheila's wedding, we watched the bride and groom share their dance; they finished, we all clapped, some people cried, then the DJ shouted for everyone to join them, so we did, everyone on the dance floor, throwing some shapes, and roughly two minutes later, everyone (including the new bride and groom) stopped, just to watch Dominic. And not because he was good. Trust me. It was crazy. Wherever the beat was, Dominic was nowhere near it. He looked like he was trying to wrestle a ghost.

So, knowing this and being handed a poster advertising me and Dominic 'The Ghost Wrestler' Clarke as a dance duo that he thought was going to win the end-of-year talent show, you can imagine my response.

I looked straight at my oldest friend and calmly said, 'Are you mad?'

But, before he could respond, Marcia Brown & Lucy Cheung were standing next to our table, staring right at me.

10

MARCIA BROWN & LUCY CHEUNG

Sometimes, two people almost seem to occupy the same space.

Like each of them is just half of one larger, more powerful being. Trying to picture one without the other is like trying to picture a head without a face, or a bird without wings. You can do it, but it's really hard and, to be honest, it feels weird.

That's what these two were like. From the very first day of reception, I honestly have no recollection of ever seeing Marcia without Lucy, or vice versa.

Even now, as I write this, I'm saying their names out loud as though it is one long name rather than two: MarciaBrownandLucyCheung.

Marcia had hair that shot out of her head like

curly, bark-coloured streamers.

Lucy's hung just above her shoulders like shiny black ribbon.

They had matching trainers. Matching coats. Matching bags. And matching frowns. They'd do this thing when you were speaking, where they'd look at each other and pout, then look right at you and shake their heads, which meant they didn't approve.

As the coolest girls in school, they had the power to make or break the reputation and social standing of anyone, teachers included.

They skipped around the school, steps fully synchronized, filling everyone they came close to with a combination of complete adulation and stone-cold dread.

If Marcia & Lucy gave you the thumbs up, it felt like someone had coloured you in with a highlighter pen. And if they gave you the thumbs down, you felt like you'd been sent to the corner.

Now here they were, standing right next to our table, staring down at me.

I quickly pushed the Full Force drawing back towards Dominic and smiled the least nervous smile I could manage.

Marcia & Lucy didn't even acknowledge Dom. They kept their eyes on me and said, 'Is it true? About your dad?'

Dominic looked at me, then at them, and started to say, 'What? Of course it's n—'

But I stopped him by cutting in.

'Yeah,' I said, looking up at them and ignoring my oldest friend. 'Yeah. It's true.'

There was a weird kind of pause, during which I tried to ignore the confused look Dominic was giving me and concentrate on Marcia & Lucy. They looked at each other and pouted, then turned to me and, speaking at exactly the same time, said:

'That's pretty cool.'

Then they both smiled, turned and walked away.

Question:

Have you ever had two girls (who happen to be super cool) speak to you at exactly the same time?

If you have, you'll understand. It does something to your brain. A kind of cross between an electric shock and a massage.

I couldn't believe it. That just happened. In the busy lunch hall. In front of Dominic. And everyone else. Marcia Brown & Lucy Cheung thought I was cool. The coolest girls in school! It was like my body was floating up out of my seat.

My brain felt like it was swimming in candyfloss. I almost couldn't breathe. 'They think I'm cool,' I said.

'What?' said Dom.

I could almost taste the words as I repeated them. 'They think I'm cool.'

Dom's face wrinkled up. 'Who does? The girls? Who cares?'

But I did. I cared.

The coolest girls in school thought I was cool. Me! Because of something that I made up about Dad . . .

. . . something that wasn't true.

I felt the cold fingers of panic slip around my throat and start to squeeze. It wasn't true. What if they asked questions? *Tighter.* Wanted details? *Tighter.* Answers that I didn't have? They'd find out. *Tighter.* That I made it up. *Tighter.* And I'd be some stupid kid who made up a stupid story to try and be cool. *No air.* I'd be torn to shreds like a teddy bear in a tiger pit. *Can't breathe.*

No.

I couldn't let that happen. If people thought it was true, I had to be sure it felt that way.

I had to research Australia and other places. I had to know loads about everywhere, so that if anyone asked me about Dad's mission and where he was, I would have an answer.

I looked at Dom.

'Library. I need to go to the library.'

'What for?'

'Research.'

'About what?'

'Australia. Dad's mission.'

'But it's not true. Why did you make that up anyway?'

'I dunno. I need to go.'

Dom shrugged. 'Cool. I'll come with you.'

But looking at him, I knew he didn't get it. He didn't feel what I felt. In Dom's world, being cool didn't matter. He didn't care what people thought. He stood up.

'We can start planning for Full Force while we're there.'

In Dom's detached-from-reality world, we were going to spend five weeks perfecting a dance routine and then get on stage in front of the whole school on the last day and actually win the talent show. Ludicrous.

I stood up and shook my head. 'No, Dom. I'm going by myself.'

11

Has your school got a library?

Maybe you have a library not too far from your house? Maybe you have a library actually in your house, I don't know. (If you do, by the way, that's crazy.)

I think libraries are incredible.

They're like secret, magical treasure rooms hidden in plain view. Shelves and shelves full of gateways to other worlds, kept in order by strange, magical creatures called librarians who, when they get to know you, somehow know exactly the kind of book you love. I still don't know why Marvel hasn't created a supernatural superhero called 'The Librarian'. They could basically call on any power of any character from any book ever. The evil bad guy could be the monster who's closing libraries down and turning them into expensive gyms.

I'd watch that movie.

It's funny though because, for some people, libraries are torture.

For some people, the library is a dusty old place where an old woman who seems to hate human beings tells you to whisper or get out.

If you're not a library person, that's OK. But if you've never been in one, I can recommend it.

Our school library was a light, open-plan

space next to the staffroom. It had a thin lime-green carpet and smelt of furniture polish and quiet. Our librarian's name was Thelma. She was like that auntie who sneakily gives you a fiver when your mum isn't watching.

Me and Dom spent a lot of lunchtimes there. Sometimes we'd help Thelma shelve books or order new stock, but most days, we'd just sit and reread old comics, debating who was the best superhero. Dom said Spider-Man, but anybody who gives it any real thought knows the correct answer is the Incredible Hulk.

One of our favourite things to do in there was read the *Guinness Book of World Records*, looking for the weird or funny ones. Do you know how big the biggest cookie ever made in the whole world was? Have a guess.

You wouldn't believe it. You can look it up later.

Let's just say you'd need a lot of milk to go with it.

(Feel free to take a biscuit break here. I am.)

So that lunchtime, when I got to the library, it was empty.

Nothing unusual about that.

Thelma was probably eating her sandwiches in her cupboard office. I headed straight to the Geography section to find a book on Australia to research details in case anyone asked me questions about Dad and his 'mission'.

And then something stopped me dead in my tracks.

Him.

Sitting there, in the corner. Face buried in a book. So engrossed he didn't even look up.

Danny Jones.

In the library.

Whatever the opposite of a 'library person' is, Danny Jones would've been the king of them. But there he was. And I couldn't believe it.

I didn't even know he knew where the library was. Not once had I ever seen him in that room and, standing there silently that lunchtime, it felt a little bit like the universe had cracked. Then fear started to fill my body like ice-water.

This wasn't good.

Danny Jones had a reputation. The tough-guy character he had crafted for himself was clear, and it did not involve me catching him in the library by himself at lunchtime. He would have absolutely no problem erasing me from existence to avoid anyone finding out. I knew I should run, but my feet wouldn't move. It was like my curiosity had more control over my body than my fear.

Then he looked up and saw me.

Our eyes met and my stomach fell into my feet. Convinced I was about to die, I froze as he started to stand.

Then I noticed the title of the book in his hand.

I looked at the book, then at him.

He looked at the book, then at me. Right at me. And said:

'Is it true, about your dad?'

His face was stone-cold serious. My mouth

felt as dry as a pharaoh's sock and the ticking in my stomach was back. Low down, behind my belly button. What to say? What the hell was happening? My hands slid into my pockets and my fingertips dug into my thighs.

I managed to force a swallow.

'Yeah, Danny,' I said. 'It is.'

12

He wanted to know everything.

Exactly where Dad was. Where he planned to go to next. How long he stayed in each place. And more than anything, he wanted to help.

Danny Jones . . . wanted to help me, help Dad on his 'mission'.

Danny Jones! The boy who, one time, poured a whole tub of glue into my PE bag and gave me a wedgie. The boy who, at the Year 5 disco, threatened to actually fold me in half and put me in the bins behind the bike sheds. He wanted to help me, help Dad with his writing mission.

I couldn't believe it.

We sat at one of the little round tables and spent the whole of lunchtime talking. I made up details about Dad and how his mission worked. The weird thing was, it kind of didn't even feel like pretending. Words just kept falling out of my mouth like some part of me believed them. Danny sucked up all the details like a hoover, and then, before I knew what was happening, he was speaking, sharing things, like a regular human being.

Here's what I learned:

1. **Danny Jones's dream** was to travel the world. He'd never been out of the country, but he had a list of places on his bedroom wall that he planned to go to when he was old enough. Top of that list? You guessed it. **Australia.**

2. **Turned out, Danny's dad had left too.** When he was in Year 2. He lived with his mum and older brother in the flats halfway between our house and school.

3. **His birthday was 18 September.** The same day as Donna's.

4. **He was a dog person.** They had a Jack Russell at home called Razor.

5. **His mum was a nurse. Just like mine.** In fact she worked in the exact same hospital!

My head was swimming.

All this stuff I had in common with Danny Jones. Unbelievable. Something about him telling me his dad had left felt like it changed things. Like it somehow made him look different. Move different. Less like a celebrity and more like . . . me?

Anyway, it was, at the time, easily the most surreal lunch hour of my life.

At one point, Thelma came in, took one look at Danny and me sitting together, and fell over the photocopier.

When the bell went, me and Danny walked back to class side by side. People couldn't believe their eyes. They kept doing double-takes and bumping into walls as they stared at us.

Whispers of 'Why are they together?' and 'What the hell is going on?' floated past us and, if I'm honest, it felt amazing. Like whatever magic cool dust he'd been sprinkled with was rubbing off on me. I was walking side by side with 'the' Danny Jones. Football captain. Tough guy. And just because I was next to him, I was cool.

I can still remember Dominic's face, when me and Danny walked back into class together. It looked like he was trying to chew a scorpion. There's me, Jason Gardner, his oldest friend, walking next to the evil super-villain kid who had terrorized us since the infants. But I knew stuff now. New stuff about Danny that made things different. Made it cool.

'Yo!' Dom said, leaning over, trying to whisper as everyone sat down for afternoon register. 'Since when are you friends with Danny Jones?'

I watched my oldest friend trying (and failing) to compute this new information, and shrugged. The pair of us looked across the room at Danny, who gave me a thumbs up and a smile. Dom nearly fell off his chair. I held a thumb up to Danny and leaned back in my seat like I'd watched him do a million times.

'Don't worry, Dom,' I said. 'It's cool.'

13

That evening, at home, sitting at the dinner table, things felt different.

This might sound stupid, but I felt bigger. Like I'd grown.

All afternoon in class, people had been watching me, whispering to themselves, smiling and nodding at me like they wanted me to smile back. At one point I got up to sharpen my pencil and, when I'd finished, it felt like the whole room almost gave me a round of applause.

I smiled to myself, as Bob Marley sang about three little birds through the living-room stereo speakers.

'Are you OK, love?' asked Mum, glancing at Donna for back-up.

I could tell they sensed something was different, but they had no idea about my day.

I figured they were waiting for more questions from me about Dad. Maybe another tantrum. But I just sat there, crafting a fish-finger Australia in a sea of garden peas. My new-found power hidden under my skin.

'Jay?' asked Mum, smiling kindly.

I smiled back and nodded. 'I'm fine.'

'How was your day?' said Donna, in that voice that teachers use when you fall over and cut your knee. I got flashes of standing in front of the class. Walking with Danny. Marcia & Lucy smiling at me.

'Yeah. Fine,' I said, stabbing the Great Barrier Reef with my fork.

Mum reached across and touched my hand. 'Sweetheart. We know this is a tricky time. We understand you have questions.'

But the truth of it was, right then, at that moment, I didn't.

I wasn't thinking about where Dad was, or why he had gone. I knew. He was in Australia, on a secret writing mission that needed my help.

82

Yes, that was my made-up truth, but after what had happened at school, it felt like enough for right now. I wasn't thinking about being angry. About being left out of the 'grown-up' facts. All I was thinking about was how cool I felt. How Danny's cool had rubbed off on me and made everyone else look at me differently. I looked across at Dad's chair in the corner. Empty and untouched since he left.

'It's OK, Mum,' I said. 'I'm cool.'

The two of them exchanged a brief, confused look, then decided to let that be the end of it for the time being. Then Mum clapped her hands. 'I need cake!' she said, and went into the kitchen.

Donna finished her juice, smiled, then started to clear the table.

'You don't have to pretend, you know,' she

said, and for one scary second I thought she might know everything. That she might somehow be able to read my mind and see what had happened at school. Then she rubbed my head. 'It's OK not to be fine, soldier.'

She didn't know. She was just trying to be a good big sister.

'OK,' I said, trying to look troubled. 'Thanks.'

Later that night, when it felt like everyone was asleep, I sat on the end of my bed in my pyjamas, staring up at my wall. At the map that Dad had put there. Light from my lamp made it look like some old cave painting. Gus was snoozing in his spot under the radiator.

I thought about Danny. How excited he'd got as we talked in the library. I thought about Marcia Brown & Lucy Cheung, standing next to our table. Everyone's eyes on me.

I heard Mr Bukowski's velvety voice: 'Thank you very much.'

I took a black felt tip from my desk and drew a black circle around Sydney. The pen tip squeaked against the laminated surface.

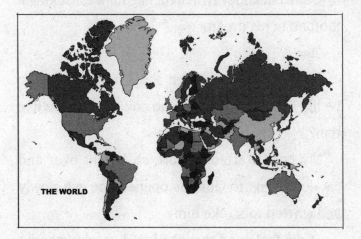

THE WORLD

I sat back down on my bed and stared at the world. I could feel Dad. A memory of watching him as he sat, where I was sitting right now, and made up stories, out of nothing. Just looking at the place I'd pointed to and running with it. And that's when it hit me.

Was I like him? I'd made up a story, out of nothing, and people liked it. Is this what Dad felt when he made up his stories? Is this why he did it? To feel cool? I looked at Gus, snoring happily under my radiator.

'Am I like him, Gus?'

Gus's back foot twitched, like he was kicking a football in his dream.

'Am I?'

I didn't know how I felt about it. Did I want to be like Dad? Somebody who could just leave like that?

My head started to hurt, so I went over and sat down next to Gus. He opened one eye slowly as I started to stroke him.

'It did feel good though,' I said, thinking about my day. Feeling cool. And I wanted more.

That's when the ticking in my stomach started again.

An idea sprouting up from deep inside.

Of course.

I stood up, staring at my map.

It was so clear what I had to do.

★★★★★★★ MY PLAN ★★★★★★★

If they thought I was cool because of one story I'd made up, I'd make up more. And the more I made up, the cooler I'd get. That could be how it worked. Simple equation: More Stories = More Cool. I had five weeks of school left. How cool could I get in five weeks? How good would that feel?

My skin started tingling. Gus let out a small, sleepy groan.

I nodded.

'You're right. I'll have to be clever. Not get caught out. Meticulous.'

I said the word again. 'Meticulous.' It felt like I was reciting a spell.

I could be meticulous.

I'd keep a record of what I made up, here, on my wall. I'd write what I'd said and who I'd said it to up on the map so I wouldn't forget. I could check my map every night to refresh my memory before I went to sleep. If I kept a record of everything I made up, I could refer to it at any time and nobody would catch me out. What an amazing idea.

Foolproof.

What could go wrong?

I clapped my hands in celebration. 'What could go wrong? Right, Gus?'

Gus didn't move.

'Gus. Are you listening? Meticulous. Cool. Brilliant plan, eh?'

Gus opened one eye to look at me . . .

. . . and farted.

Pause.

❀
❀

I know what you're thinking.

Or, rather, I know what I think you're thinking.

I think you're thinking: *I agree with Gus, Jay. In fact, if I could fart right now, and send it to where you are, I would. That is a terrible plan. A real stinker. Have you never read old fairy tales? Do you not remember the one with the boy crying wolf and all the sheep that got eaten and then he got eaten and had to live with the old guy inside the wolf's belly?* Maybe that's not how it goes, I can't remember the exact details, but I hear what you're saying. The moral of the story is, don't tell lies or you'll end up in someone's belly. You'll think you're being clever, but it can end up badly. Yeah yeah yeah.

But I always thought the characters in those old stories were pretty stupid, really. They always let things get out of control. I wouldn't. I would be smart enough to take things just as far as I wanted to, and stop when it was time. I was in control enough to decide how things would end.

Maybe this story should've ended right there. With Gus looking at me and saying, 'Don't do it. Who cares about being cool? Just enjoy your last few weeks of Year 6 before the summer. Now go to sleep.' A little fart, and then . . .

THE END

But that's not what happened.

See, ideas are powerful. I didn't understand just how powerful back then, but I do now.

Sometimes an idea can overtake you. Sometimes an idea can grow so big inside your brain that it blocks out other stuff. Facts. Truth. Your ability to see what might be coming. All just to make sure it gets its own way. I understand it better now, trust me.

Ideas can have their own life. And the idea of being cool and getting cooler had planted itself firmly in the centre of my brain and started to grow roots. I would get cooler and cooler and stop having to waste time thinking about Dad.

More Stories = More Cool = Less Dad = Winning.

And as I finally climbed into bed that night, I was ready to be the coolest winner the world had ever seen.

Week One

14

Walking into school with Dominic on the Tuesday, I felt like I had springs in my shoes. I was so charged up to put my plan into action, I hadn't really noticed how quiet Dom was being. Dom was never quiet on the walk to school. As we passed the old church, I turned to him.

'Why aren't you talking?'

Dom looked down.

'My mum told me about your dad.'

I felt something heavy in my stomach, but made myself keep walking.

'Is he really gone?' Dom said, sheepishly looking my way.

I got a flash of Danny's face from the day before in the library.

'Yep,' I said, staring forward, trying to keep all emotion out of my voice. I could feel Dom's eyes on me as we approached the corner.

'Do you want to talk about it?' he said.

I cooly shook my head. 'Nah. I'm fine.'

As we turned on to the road school was on, I spotted a couple of Year 5 girls on scooters looking at me like I was famous. One of them waved at me. I waved back. They both giggled.

Dom put his hand on my shoulder. 'Jay, you're allowed to be sad.'

I could feel something in my throat. I swallowed it.

'I'm fine, man. Seriously. Now, don't we have a talent show to plan for?'

It was like the words snapped him back into normal Dom mode, bursting the tension of the moment, and I breathed a sigh of relief as he dived into his ideas.

'We need to choose a song,' he said. 'Something powerful, but funky. I was thinking last night, and I reckon James Brown. What's that one with the saxophones at the start, the one from Sheila's wedding?'

He pulled out a little notebook and pencil like a detective from an old film.

'Jay?'

I shrugged.

'"Cold Sweat"?'

Dominic grinned. 'Yes!' He made a note, then chewed the end of his pencil. 'I reckon my dad will have it somewhere.' He checked himself. 'Sorry. I didn't mean to mention . . .'

He was squirming because he'd said the word 'dad', like that was somehow a word he wasn't allowed to use around me, and it was annoying. Like a person who wasn't even here could still have a power over things.

'Forget it,' I said. 'I'm not even thinking about him.'

Which was actually true. My mind was already thinking of story ideas. Dom put his notebook away. 'We need to draw up a rehearsal schedule. I'll do it. Five weeks is tight, but if we get on it, we'll be fine. We are winning that thing, Jay. Trust me.'

As we walked through the school gates it felt

like most of the other kids turned to watch me. Like in those old western films where a mysterious stranger walks into the saloon. That was me. New Jason. Cool Jason.

Dom didn't even notice. But I did. I put on my coolest 'not really bothered' face and walked to class line-up. My plan was already working and I hadn't even opened my mouth.

Here's the thing.

If I listed all of the stories I made up over the following five weeks, this book would be 50,000 pages long and weigh as much as an elephant who loves McDonald's. If I typed up every single thing I told people during that time you'd still be reading this when you are old and wrinkly, and your great-grandchildren are running around playing with their virtual reality unicorns.

So I won't.

I'll just pick a few at random from the VERY LONG list and share them as we go along.

For example:

WEEK 1. Tuesday. Morning Break.
Back Playground:
'Me vs Mickey Mouse'

Georgette Foster was telling everyone by the climbing frame that she was going to Disneyland in the summer holidays with her family. I told her (and everyone else gathered round) that, when I was eight, me and my family went to Euro Disney near Paris and stayed in one of the log cabins. I said it was lots of fun and we were having a great time, eating giant pretzels, riding on roller coasters and stuff, until we got thrown out by security because I punched Mickey Mouse in the face.

'What?' people said.

'No way!' people said.

'It's true,' I said. 'We were taking a photo and Mickey Mouse kept tickling me and I was telling him to stop and he wouldn't and I got really angry and he kept tickling and then something came over me and I jumped up and smacked Mickey Mouse in his massive mouse head and it fell off and the man inside the costume looked at us like all his clothes had just disappeared, and ran away.'

'Really?'

'Yep.'

They believed me.

To this day, I've never been to Euro Disney.

But I'd seen it on TV plenty of times, and I knew who Mickey Mouse was, so when Georgette started talking I just let the film of me fighting Mickey Mouse play out in my mind and my mouth described it out loud.

People were leaning forward, hanging off the monkey bars as I spoke.

I felt like the centre of the universe.

15

Standing in the queue for lunch, holding my tray, everything felt different. Colours. Sounds. Things felt brighter. Clearer. Better. It was like up until then I'd been wearing sunglasses and headphones my whole school life and now I'd taken them off.

Sitting in our usual spots near the gym apparatus, I did my best with the dry school potatoes and rubbery gravy while Dom made more notes in his little pad about Full Force and thought aloud.

'If I can get Noah to lend us his boombox, we can practise in the garage, or the park. We'll need batteries, though. Can you backflip?'

'No, Dom, I can't backflip. And neither can you.'

'Not yet,' he said with a grin. Then Danny Jones sat down right next to him.

Dominic went rigid as Danny sniffed, and stabbed his juice carton with the straw.

'All right?' he said.

Dominic looked at me, like a dog trapped inside a car. I ate another potato and nodded.

'Yeah. You?'

Danny sucked on his straw until the empty carton folded into itself, then he crushed it on the table like a Viking finishing his tankard of ale. 'I've been thinking.'

He looked at Dominic, who seemed to shrink into his own shoulders, then at me.

'I'm good at research.'

I nodded calmly. 'OK.'

Dominic made a noise that was half cough and half yelp, then put his notepad away.

'I'm gonna . . . I just . . . I said I'd help Mr Bukowski with a thing.' He stood up, careful not to bump shoulders with Danny. 'Good chatting with you.' He gave me a quick 'What the hell is going on?' stare, then he left, almost falling into the bin as he emptied his tray.

Danny slid over into Dom's seat. 'If you find out where he's going to next, I can research it for him, so he's got info,' he said. 'Then you can read it to him when he calls you. So he's prepared.'

There was a strange expression on his face that didn't seem to fit. Like the muscles weren't used to making it. Looking at him, I realized what it was. It was hope. Danny Jones was hoping I thought his idea was good. I felt the air filling my lungs as I sat up straight and said, 'That'd be great.'

Danny Jones smiled, and for a second, I thought he was going to flip the lunch table over in excitement. He composed himself, then just stared at me. I nodded. He stared expectantly.

'Oh,' I said, eventually realizing what he was waiting for. 'Sorry. Japan. He's going to Japan.' The place had just popped into my head. I nodded with more certainty. 'Yep. Tokyo. He wrote me a letter. He flies this weekend.'

'A letter?'

'I know. He's a writer. Don't ask.' I had no idea

where that came from, but it worked.

Danny Jones nodded once, like a samurai who's just been given a mission.

'I'm on it,' he said, in a stone-cold serious voice. And he started eating his potatoes.

And that's what we decided. Our routine.

Danny, helping me, helping Dad. Like a team.

Every Monday, I would bring in a letter from Dad. (There hadn't been a single letter, message or anything from him since he left. I would have to write them myself, but I would keep them short and as long as I switched up my handwriting, I'd be fine.) The fake letter would say where Dad was planning on going to next for his writing mission. I'd bring the letter to school, show it to Danny and then he would spend the

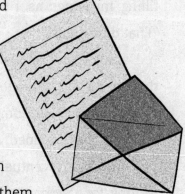

rest of the week preparing a report on that place. Important locations, historical facts, population, things that I could then relay to Dad when I spoke to him.

I can't even take credit for coming up with the idea, to be honest, it was all Danny's. All I did was go along with it and fake the letters. Danny got so excited about researching places around the world it almost felt like I'd given him a gift. He spent less time giving people grief because he was too busy, so I kind of gave them a gift too. Some of the football gang got annoyed because they lost their best player for most lunchtimes to the library, of all places. None of it was real, but it was to him, and he loved it.

A purpose for his passion.

What could be wrong with that?

16

Walking home that afternoon, I was going over the things I'd made up.

- Punching Mickey Mouse.
- Dad's letter.

Before home time we'd been talking in class about heritage and family histories. Mum's side of the family are from Jamaica. Her mum and dad came over in the 1960s looking for work. Mum was born here, but she used to go to Jamaica a lot when she was younger, before she had her own family. I'd never even been to Jamaica, but I'd seen lots of photos and heard stories, so when Mr Bukowski was asking about where people's families came from, I told him, and everyone else, that I was born in Jamaica. Everyone was impressed, so I took it further. I told them I was actually born in an area called Nine Mile, which is where Bob Marley was born. I knew this from Mum talking about it. People were even more impressed by that. Mr Bukowski too.

'That's a pretty special fact,' he said, in his super-silky calm voice. And I beamed like the cat that got the cream.

- Nine Mile.

I would write them all up on my map when I got home. Two days in. Things were going great.

Then Dominic caught me up, out of breath.

'Yo! Why didn't you wait for me?'

He leaned on me, panting.

'Sorry. I forgot.' The words felt weird coming out of my mouth. Different to almost all the others I'd spoken that day. They were the truth.

Luckily Dominic wasn't really paying attention.

'Two minutes and fifty-five seconds, Part One,' he said, starting to breathe normally again.

'Three minutes and fifty-five seconds, Part Two.'

'What?'

'"Cold Sweat" by James Brown. That's six minutes and fifty seconds in total.'

'Oh. OK. Is that good?'

'No! That's way too long to dance to. We'll have to use just one part. I say Part One, that's the most funky, right?'

'I guess.'

Dom winced. 'Two minutes and fifty-five seconds. That's still a pretty long time to dance for. Lot of choreography.'

'Maybe we shouldn't bother then,' I said.

Dominic looked down his nose at me, then laughed and punched my arm. 'Good one, Jay. Always joking.'

He started walking, already gesticulating wildly as he described dance moves he'd heard about from Miss Grego, who led the after school dance club. I let him get a few steps ahead, then followed, feeling like me and my best friend were two trains on very different tracks.

17

The rest of that first week flew by.

I made up more stories each day. The map on my wall was starting to fill up.

Dominic threw himself into Full Force preparations for the talent show and Danny Jones was busy researching Tokyo for Dad.

Home started to feel more like an empty train station.

Mum was doing more shifts at the hospital, which meant that most of the time she was home she was sleeping. By the time I got back from school she was either already out, or her bedroom door was closed, which meant Do Not Disturb.

Donna was supposed to be 'watching' me while Mum worked, but most days she was out with her friends until dinner time, and then, when she was home, she only ever seemed to be in the shower or shut in her room with her music. That meant most of the time it was just me and Gus, which would maybe have felt more lonely if I hadn't had new stories to revise and remember every night before I went to sleep.

I don't know the exact numbers, but by Thursday night of that first week I already had to juggle more than twenty different made-up stories and their details in my head. Now, whether you think that's a good idea or not, you have to admit, it's kind of impressive.

Could you do it?

WEEK 1. Thursday. PE Lesson.
The Pitch:
'Mutant Me'

Paul Benton was talking about the X-Men in the playground.

He was saying how Wolverine's body can regenerate from any injury and how cool it would be to have a genetic mutation that gave you a power. Everyone started arguing about what would be the best power to have. I knew that saying I had an actual full-on power would be too much, but an idea popped into my head and I went with it.

Here's what I said. As an experiment, try reading this next bit out loud, following the directions as you go, so you do exactly what I did, and see how it feels.

'You know I was born with six fingers on my left hand? Well, five fingers and a thumb.' **Hold out your left hand and stroke the base of your little finger. Don't stop talking though.** 'Up until I was two I had nine fingers and two thumbs, then when I was two I had an operation to have it taken off. Mum said it was for the best because people might tease me. Dad said I should've kept it and learned the piano. I could've been like some kind of classical maestro or something.' **Hold your hand out further for people to try and see, but keep a finger in the**

way and maintain eye contact. 'Yeah, if you look closely, you can still see a scar.' **Put your hand back down and shrug.**

'No way!' they'll say.

Just nod.

'Is that true?' they'll ask.

Nod again and say: 'Crazy, right?'

They believed me.

Would they believe you?

It is amazing what people will believe if you say it like you mean it.

On Friday morning when everyone was hanging up their coats, Danny Jones came over holding a brown card folder. The beam of pride on his face practically gave off heat. I looked at the cover. In tall handwritten letters it said:

'I think it's good,' he said, smiling. I took the file and opened the first page:

SUMMARY

OFFICIAL TITLE: TOKYO METROPOLIS.

* JAPANESE CAPITAL SINCE 1869.
* 39 MILLION RESIDENTS.
* 50% MORE PEOPLE THAN ANY OTHER URBAN AREA IN THE WORLD.
* $2.5 TRILLION ECONOMY, LARGER THAN ANY OTHER CITY.
* RANKED NO.1 SAFEST CITY IN THE WORLD FOR THE PAST FIVE YEARS.

Behind the first pages there were more pages, with drawings of bullet trains, graphs about the population breakdown and diagrams about money and food. It was really impressive. I nodded and closed the file.

'Good work,' I said.

Danny grinned. 'I hope he likes it.'

And as I looked at him, just for half a second, I felt something on my shoulder. The briefest tap from a tiny finger of guilt. I looked down and it went away.

At lunchtime Danny asked me to play football with him and some of the others. I felt like a gazelle running around with lions. Dean McPike and Jordan Sancho from the other Year 6 class kept kicking me, letting me know they weren't keen on me being in the game but, whenever I got fouled, Danny would charge over and square up to whoever kicked me and they'd back down. It was like I had my own bodyguard enforcer.

At one point I went in goal and as the game carried on I looked up at the staffroom window and saw Mr Bukowski looking down. I was about to wave, then the ball crashed into the fence next to my head, starting cheers for the goal, and when I looked up again, the window was empty.

19

When the bell went for the end of the day, a little part of me was glad I would have the weekend to recharge. It had only been a week, but my late-night revision sessions already had me feeling more tired than usual.

Homework was just spelling, so at least that was one less thing to have to think about.

As we packed our bags, Dominic handed me another piece of paper with a handwritten timetable on it:

SATURDAY: Team discussion. listening session and brainstorming.
SUNDAY: Core strength and muscle work.
MONDAY: Choreography.
TUESDAY: Rehearsal.
WEDNESDAY: Rehearsal.
THURSDAY: Rehearsal.
FRIDAY: Rest and recovery.   **REPEAT.**

'Four weeks, Jay. Gonna be tight.'

His face was deadly serious. Full Force was really a thing to him. It felt like there was a gap between us. Like Dom was on one pavement and I was across the road.

'This seems like a lot, Dom,' I said, hoping he would read between the lines and see that I wasn't keen at all. He didn't, of course. Like I said, ideas are powerful, and Dominic's vision of us winning the talent show was playing in full HD in his mind.

'You want to come to mine tonight?' he said as we left the classroom. 'Noah's got some old James Brown TV performance recorded. We can make notes.'

'I can't,' I said, without even thinking. 'We're going out for dinner.'

We weren't. Mum was still on nights.

'Maybe tomorrow then,' he said. 'Oh, and Mum said to let you know we're not doing a party for my birthday this year. Just a little get-together at ours and –' he paused for dramatic effect – 'a cake-eating contest!'

He grinned and rubbed his stomach, waiting for me to get excited.

Then Danny Jones caught us up, holding something. It was his file.

'You forgot this!'

He held it out like the Olympic torch. I must've left it on my desk. I smacked my forehead with my palm to show how stupid I was. Dominic looked everywhere else but at Danny. I took the folder, hours of his work that I'd forgotten all about.

'Silly me. Lot on my mind. Thanks, Danny.'

'It's all right. Don't forget his new letter on Monday though, OK?'

Dom looked at me. I avoided his eyes and stayed on Danny. 'Course not. I'll have it. Promise.'

We exchanged nods and Danny jogged off to catch up with Dean and the others.

Dominic looked at Danny's file. I stuck it into my bag and said nothing, then me and my oldest friend walked home pretty much in silence, a thick cloud of what we weren't saying out loud following us all the way.

20

A room full of people.

Mum, Donna, me, Dominic, Nana, Grandad, Uncle Michael, Aunt Marie, all the cousins and second cousins, Mr Bukowski, Gus, Bob Marley, Bruce Lee, Einstein. There's music playing. It's James Brown, 'Cold Sweat'. In fact, James Brown is there, with Wolverine and Diego Maradona, Mickey Mouse, Santa, the Queen, Marcia Brown & Lucy Cheung. Danny Jones, Dean and Jordan, loads of little reception and Year 1 kids are there too and, in the corner, in his chair, Dad.

Everyone is mingling and chatting, eating little buffet snacks, but Dad is just sitting there, in his chair, staring at me through the crowd.

I'm smiling and nodding along with people. It's my party. In our house. I recognize the wallpaper, but it's bigger. Like our living room has grown into a hall. And now I'm moving. Not walking, but kind of floating, between people, towards Dad.

It's like he's pulling me towards him in some kind of invisible tractor beam. People are moving to let me through, and I'm getting closer and closer, and Dad's just staring at me. Closer and closer, and I'm warm. In my stomach. Like I've just eaten a big bowl of chicken soup. And I'm floating to him. Close enough so I'm almost reaching him. Santa is the last person between us. His big red and white body starts to move, and for a second Dad disappears behind him, then as Santa steps to the side, Dad is gone. Disappeared. And it's just his chair.

Empty.

❁

I woke up with a headache.

The house was early-morning quiet. I rolled on to my side and saw Gus sleeping under my radiator. 'Morning,' I said. Gus sneezed.

I lay back and stared up at my wall. There were black circles around several different cities and scribbled notes in the Pacific Ocean. I tried to remember the last place I had pointed to for Dad to make up a story about before he'd left, but I couldn't. I stretched out my arm and pointed my finger towards Africa, then South America, Antarctica. Looking for a memory.

'Where are you, Dad?'

My finger hovered, wandering like one of those sticks they use to find water, then it stopped. I got up, following the line of my point and touched the map.

❦

Dear Jason,

Things are going well. It is hectic, but the information in your report on Tokyo really helped. Please thank your friend Danny for me. I am leaving to go to Borneo at the end of the week. Any details you can find out would be a big help.

Speak soon.

Dad

Week Two

21

Danny read the letter all the way through, twice, in front of me, and I watched the lights come on in the top floor of his brain.

'It's an island, right?' he said.

'I think so, yeah?'

'Cool.'

We were in the cloakroom before first bell. Dominic had made his excuses and headed for class as soon as Danny approached us. I watched Danny tuck the letter into his bag like it was a priceless artefact and we headed to class.

Dom was already in his seat when we walked in. Marcia Brown & Lucy Cheung were talking about a gymnastics competition they'd won at the weekend and Dom was listening keenly like a news reporter.

I sat down in my seat just as Mr Bukowski came in.

Dom pointed towards Marcia & Lucy.

'They're gonna be our main competition,' he said.

I had to stop myself rolling my eyes. I'd spent the whole of Saturday afternoon with him, watching Noah's old James Brown video over and over, and biting my tongue while he tried to copy the moves in his living room. I'm not saying it was a painful experience, but let's just say I wasn't inspired with confidence at our chances.

'Dom, I think we need to get real.'

Dom nodded. 'Exactly. Hard work, hard work and more hard work. That's our reality if we really want this.'

That wasn't what I meant. At all. But before I could say that, Mr Bukowski stood up and said, 'Dinosaurs are alive! And they live amongst us!'

Week 2. Monday. First Lesson.
Classroom:
'Hunting Morris'

We were learning about reptiles.

How some of them have been around since the last dinosaurs roamed the earth. At the end of the lesson, everyone was talking about which was more scary, a crocodile or a cobra.

We'd learned how fast a crocodile can be on land and how if one is chasing you, you should run in a zigzag pattern as they struggle to change direction and it confuses them. When Jonathan Davies told everyone he'd seen an adder in the woods when he'd visited his grandad in Devon, people seemed impressed. I seized the moment and told everyone that my Uncle Tony had a pet boa constrictor called Morris, and that one time we went to stay with Uncle Tony and the first night we were there, Morris went missing. We spent the whole weekend looking for Morris, worried about what he could get up to in the neighbourhood, then when we finally found him, curled up under next door's shed, Morris had a smile on his face and lump in his stomach roughly the same size and shape as next door's cat.

'Eurgh! Is that true?' they said.

'Yep,' I said.

'That's so gross!' they said.

'I know,' I said.

They believed me.

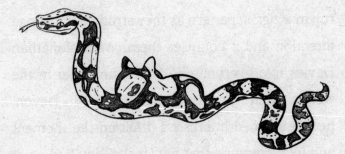

22

The days started to fall into a pattern. I was making up on average roughly ten or eleven stories a day. Some of them were small and throwaway. Little exaggerations thrown out into someone else's conversation that wouldn't need much afterthought.

Example: 'Oh yeah, my sister does kung fu as well. One time she forearm-chopped a shoplifter in Sainsbury's and got a certificate from the police.'

Nobody would ask about that one again, but it still had to be logged.

Like I said: meticulous.

Others were bigger, closer to the main one about Dad, and needed more thought and effort.

By Wednesday of that second week, I was spending nearly an hour and a half checking my wall before bed, pacing up and down, speaking the stories out loud to Gus to fix them into my memory. Planting fake flowers amongst the real ones in the garden of my mind.

I dodged Full Force sessions when I could, making up excuses to Dom that always revolved around Donna or Mum needing me for something at home, but on Wednesday I couldn't think of something quickly enough so I had to go round.

Dom's house was way bigger than ours. Fatter. His dad, James, designs office buildings, and his mum, Frances, is a science professor at the university. I'm not quite sure how it's possible for a ten-year-old boy and a forty-three-year-old woman to look like twins, but Dom and his mum kind of did. Same mousey hair, same wide eyes and crooked smile. It was kind of amazing.

Their living room was twice the size of ours and if you sat fully back in their big green leather sofa, your feet didn't even reach the floor.

I'm not sure how many sleepovers I had there, but it was enough to feel completely fine with going to the fridge by myself to get a drink.

That Wednesday, when we got to his, he took me to their garage. Inside he'd cleared a space and put down a big square of old carpet for us to dance on. Noah's chunky silver boombox was sitting on a plastic crate and there were two hand towels folded next to it. Dom had set up our own personal dance studio.

'Right,' he said, clapping his hands together like a PE teacher. 'I think we should start with some basic footwork. Is that what you're wearing?'

I looked down at my jeans and T-shirt. 'What else would I wear?'

Dom tutted, annoyed. 'We'll get to costumes later. That'll have to do for today. Take your trainers off at least, though.'

He pressed PLAY on the tape and started doing leg stretches like an athlete as the horns of 'Cold Sweat' began to play. I couldn't help but laugh.

'It's not funny, Jay. I want this.'

'I know you do,' I said, half-heartedly copying his warm-up.

To this day, I'm grateful that nobody was filming the next two hours. Or the couple of other 'rehearsal' sessions I actually showed up for over the next couple of weeks. That footage would be prime blackmail material for sure.

Later on, sitting at their big dining table eating thick sausages and mashed potatoes with James and Frances, it struck me how long it had been since me, Mum and Donna had eaten a meal all together. Mum hadn't cooked for ages because of work and Donna just threw oven pizzas in and told me to sort myself out. We used to eat together whenever we could when Dad was around. Things in my life had really changed since half-term, and sitting here with Dom's regular family made me think about just how much.

'So how's your mum doing?' asked James. I saw Frances give him a sharp look as if to warn him off the subject, so I helped him out with a quick answer.

'She's OK. Working a lot of shifts at the hospital,' I said, scooping potatoes.

'That's good, I suppose,' said James. 'Keeping busy.' Frances cut him an even sharper look and there was an awkward pause. I looked at Dom. He could see I needed help, but he had a mouthful of sausage.

I forced a smile and carried on eating.

'I did try and call her,' said Frances, giving me the sympathy eyes. 'You're welcome over here any time you like, Jason. You know that, right?'

I nodded. 'Thank you.'

James pointed at me with his fork. 'Yep. They can be messy things sometimes, families.'

I didn't know where to look. Adults have this annoying way of making you feel like they know stuff you don't at the best of times, but when the subject is your own dad leaving, it's twenty times worse. What did they know? Had Mum spoken to Frances? Did she know more than me? Frances coughed as though some potato had gone down the wrong way. Dom had emptied his mouth, but for once in his life he couldn't think of something to say. I didn't want to deal with this at all. I'd been doing a pretty good job of not thinking about Dad, keeping busy with my stories, but James wasn't finished.

'Who knows why people do what they do, eh? Not me. Leaving your family, I mean—'

Before he could say any more, Frances shot out of her chair. 'Dancing!' she said, pointing at me and Dom. 'You boys are working on something special for the talent show, I hear?'

Dom brilliantly followed her lead and started explaining Full Force.

James looked slightly confused at the change of subject, but went back to eating. Frances sat back down, smiling awkwardly, and listened intently to Dom.

I was just glad the attention was off me and, as I cut into a sausage, I made a mental note not to come for dinner at Dom's again any time soon.

How are you doing?

A lot of words, aren't they, books?

If you've made it this far, you've read approximately 15,000 words. If each one of those words was an apple, that'd be a pretty big pile of apples, right? Too many to eat. That would probably be enough apples to fill a swimming pool and dive in. Maybe that would be painful. Yeah, I don't think diving into a swimming pool of apples is a great idea.

How about marshmallows?

15,000 football-sized marshmallows. That sounds like the kind of swimming pool I'd like to dive into. Can you eat while you swim? Would you sink?

I can think of worse things than sinking in a pool full of marshmallows, to be honest.

Great. Now I'm hungry, for marshmallows.

I'm getting distracted from the story, sorry.

That's the thing about the brain isn't it? If you just let it run, sometimes you can end up lost.

23

Danny's report on Borneo that Friday was even more thorough than his Tokyo one.

Did you know that Borneo is the third largest island in the world? Neither did I.

I made sure to put it straight into my bag this time.

Our homework for Monday was to write a page on what we thought about the future. Mr Bukowski had been talking to us about secondary school and we'd watched this little film about starting Year 7 in September. It was all about going from feeling like the biggest people in school to feeling like the smallest.

Most of us in the class were going to Wakens Tip High School together, so would still see each other, and, having never once felt like the biggest person in school, I couldn't see what was going to feel so different.

But then I realized something. I did feel bigger. Maybe I still wasn't physically the biggest kid in school, but my status had definitely grown. People ignored me way less and I definitely took up more space. The stamp of approval from Danny, and my new role as storyteller supreme, had seen to that, and feeling as cool as I did, I couldn't let my momentum slip.

In PE, while we lined up to vault over the wooden horse thing, I told Simon Harris, Mark Halpin and Chris Northall that my mum one time saved a guy's life in the big Tesco in town with some frozen crab sticks and an empty fountain pen.

'No way!' they said.

'Serious,' I said.

'Like an actual operation, with blood and stuff?' they said.

'Fully. It was all over the floor by the freezers,' I said.

They believed me.

That afternoon, while we were crossing out words in newspaper pages to make found poems, I told Heather Cunning and Catherine Onyade that scientists in North Korea had found a way to graft a great white shark's head on to a rhino's body to use in case of a ground war with the South.

'Get lost!' they said.

'It's true,' I said. 'They don't have any of the ethical regulations of the West.'

'That's disgusting. And really sad,' they said.

'I know,' I said. 'I couldn't believe it either. My mum's friend is a reporter. She told us.'

They believed me.

That night, as I stood at my map, circling places and jotting notes, I realized I'd lost count of how many things I'd made up. After I'd reached the sixties, I'd stopped counting. How many didn't matter as much as the details, and I didn't want to waste any brain space with numbers. I'd started joining up the different entries with lines to show which ones were connected. It was just two weeks after I'd started, and my wall already looked like the enormous messy scrapbook of a crazy giant.

I flopped on to my bed, exhausted, but smiling with pride.

'It's working, Gus,' I said, folding my arms behind my head. 'My brain is full to bursting, but it's working.'

Gus let out a little murmur, and when I looked down, he was sitting up, staring at me.

'What is it, boy?'

I slid on to the floor and sat next to him. Gus just stared.

'You OK?' I stroked behind his ears and he flopped into my lap.

'It's like I'm a different person,' I said as he rolled over to show me his belly. I scratched and stroked his chest as he nuzzled his nose behind my knees.

'You're still the same, though,' I said, giving

him a squeeze. 'Aren't you?'

Gus grunted and gave me a 'Just shut up and stroke me' look.

So I did. I just stroked my dog and felt the calm of my brain growing quiet as Gus fell asleep in my lap.

I slept late that Saturday morning.

By the time I woke up, the sunlight was already halfway across my room. My map was washed golden and the black pen of my scribbled notes seemed to sparkle like cat's ~~lies~~ eyes.

Lying in bed, I could hear talking through the floor. I couldn't hear actual words, but Mum and Donna were discussing something with more volume than a normal conversation. As I tuned in to try and work out what they were saying, the similarities in their voices became clear. Donna's voice was basically a slightly higher-pitched version of Mum's, which kind of made sense. I wondered if my voice sounded like a younger version of Dad's and whether I liked the idea of that or not.

Even though they were going back and forth,

Donna was speaking way more than Mum. There'd be a blast of Donna, followed by a short, calmer bit of Mum, then more Donna, for longer. It was almost like when you can half hear somebody else's tunes through their headphones on the bus.

Then there was a bang. Gus lifted his head. I tilted mine, waiting for what came next. Donna said something and then I heard heavy footsteps, followed by the front door opening and slamming shut. Then it was quiet – an empty quiet I'd almost got used to in the house over the past couple of weeks, but which right now felt wrong, and I wanted to do something about it.

Mum was sitting at the table, head in her hands. I stood in the doorway in my pyjamas for a while, not sure if she knew I was there.

'Mum?'

Mum wiped her face with the back of her hand, and I got the urge to run over and hug her.

I didn't, though. And I'm not sure why.

'Morning, sweetheart,' she said, smiling. 'How'd you sleep?'

'Fine. Are you OK?'

Mum tidied her hair. 'I will be.'

'Is Donna all right?'

Mum sighed. It was the kind of sigh that you've seen your mum do a bunch of times, I'm sure. The kind of sigh that comes when you've been carrying something heavy for a long time.

'She'll be OK,' said Mum, then she beckoned me over.

When I reached her, she stood up and held me at the shoulders.

'I think you grew,' she said.

I shrugged. Her fingers squeezed me. 'My big, big man.'

Then she pulled me in and hugged me.

Now, I'm not a hug expert. I haven't conducted any registered studies into hugs, their quality and properties or the power scale, but I would happily bet everything I own in the world on the fact that hugs from mums carry more power than any others.

Whenever I hug my mum, I feel like I'm in a time machine. I am four. I am two. I am ten. I am a newborn baby, fresh in the world. And I am safe.

I hugged her back and it felt as though we were speaking without words.

I was saying, '*I don't understand . . .*'

Mum was saying, '*I'm not going anywhere . . .*'

We stayed right there for a while, then Mum stroked my head and said, 'Let's take Gus to the woods.'

⚅

Like I said before, Gus was already seventy at this point. His usual walks were just a slow stroll-around-the-block-type deal. The park was something we used to do back in the day, all four of us together. We'd spend half the day stomping through the leaves, collecting pine cones and catapult sticks. Gus was never the 'throw-and-catch' type. When any of us threw a ball, he would just watch it arc through the air, land somewhere in the distance, and then he'd look up at you as if to say, '*What do you think is going to happen now?*'

He did used to enjoy running, though. In his younger days he was pretty fast too. He'd race around after bigger dogs and then spend some long minutes getting a good sniff of their bums and faces and having the occasional wrestle. But as he got older, the trips to the woods became less frequent. He ran around a lot less. Sometimes we'd get halfway there and he'd start walking really slowly or even just sit down in the middle of the pavement, letting you know he wasn't up to it, so we stopped taking him and just let him sleep.

When Mum grabbed the lead and did her 'We're going to the woods' wolf whistle that morning, I think Gus was just as surprised as me. He went with it, though, and as we walked along our old route to Warley Woods, I could tell by his steps that he was almost excited.

We took our time ambling through the trees,

waiting for Gus as he investigated rotting stumps and rabbit holes. At one point a young German shepherd showed up and Gus fell in love. I could see it in his eyes. They went all cloudy and his head tilted as he watched her bouncing around and chewing fallen branches. I reckon if he had hands and not paws, he might have sat down and written her a poem.

I could tell that Mum had brought me along to talk. There's a specific type of quiet that grown-ups get when there's something important to tell you and they're struggling to find the words. It's like when you press MUTE on the TV remote control. You know there's sound there, it's just not coming out right now.

As we stood by the mossy marble fountain near the pine trees, waiting for Gus to drink from the trough, Mum leaned against the stone and looked at me.

'We have to be strong, Jay,' she said.

I wanted so badly to say something that showed I was grown-up enough to hold my own in the conversation, but no words came to mind.

'People make choices,' she said. 'And those choices have consequences.'

My head started filling up with the wrong things. School. Dad's made-up mission. My map. I tried to stay in the moment, but it was like my bedroom wall was right there in front of us, demanding my attention.

'Do you know what I mean?' said Mum.

I watched Gus scamper off towards a scruffy-looking Jack Russell near the bushes.

'I think so.'

Mum took a deep breath

'See, your father and me. We—'

'Jason?'

The voice didn't fit. It was a boy's voice. Saying my name. I looked at Mum's mouth. It wasn't moving.

'Jay?'

Mum pointed over my shoulder. Danny Jones was standing there, holding a dirty white football that looked like it had been eaten and pooped out by an angry bull.

'Danny?'

It felt funny seeing him outside of school. He didn't look as ferocious. He didn't look ferocious at all.

'Hello. I'm Angela,' said Mum.

Danny looked at her. 'Hi, Angela. I'm Danny, Jason's friend from school.'

Mum looked at me. I looked at Danny. He called me his friend.

'It's Danny,' I said.

'We've established that,' said Mum as Gus and the Jack Russell came running over, tangled up like best buddies.

'And who is this?' asked Mum, squatting down to stroke the little dog.

'That's Razor,' said Danny.

Mum tickled Razor's neck, and he immediately flipped over on to his back for some belly attention.

'Razor, is it?' said Mum, scratching Razor's stomach. 'You don't seem so sharp to me.'

Danny shrugged, and it could've been the light or the fact that we were surrounded by tall trees, but I swear he was smaller.

'Did you get another letter'?' he asked, and panic jumped on to my back.

Mum looked up at me. 'Letter?'

'All good,' I said quickly. 'It hasn't arrived yet. Postman comes in the afternoon. How come you're here?'

'We come here every Saturday,' said Danny. 'Razor likes chasing the birds.'

Mum stood up and I could tell she was going to ask more about the letter. What was I going to tell her? That I was faking a letter from Dad about a secret writing mission he was on that gave Danny weekly research assignments? And admit it to Danny too? Not happening. I had to think fast.

'You wanna do something?' I said.

Danny nodded. 'OK. You wanna come back to mine?'

I looked at Mum. She'd brought me here to talk and I knew there was more she wanted to say before Danny showed up, but I had to get out of this situation before anything else got revealed. Luckily, Mum read my face and body language like only mums can.

'You go on, be with your friend. I'll take Gus home. Do you live close, Danny?'

'Biko Estate,' said Danny.

Mum put Gus's lead back on. 'Ah, that's not far at all. Just be home in time for dinner, OK, Jay?'

I nodded.

'Come on then, old man,' Mum said, ruffling Gus's ears. 'Let's get you back home.'

Gus and Razor exchanged a doggy nod, and

then Gus and Mum walked off back the way we'd come. Danny watched them until they were out of sight. Razor started sniffing my ankles like he was planning to pee on them.

'So is your dad white, then?' said Danny, turning back to me. The question kind of threw me. ''Cos you're, I mean, you're a mix, right?' he added.

'Yep,' I said, wondering why that even mattered.

Danny nodded like a grown-up. 'Cool.'

He looked kind of lost. I wanted to help him. 'We can stay here if you like,' I said. 'Build a fort or something?'

Danny shivered, like he was snapping himself out of a thought.

'Nah, it's all right,' he said. 'My mum's working till late, so we're good. I can show you my encyclopedias.'

He launched the battered football along the path and Razor darted after it.

'Let's go.'

25

Danny's flat was on the eleventh floor of one of the three tower blocks on Biko Estate.

Maybe it was because I didn't ride in lifts very often and he did it every day, but I was clearly way more hyped about pushing the buttons and the whirring noise of the cable than I should've been. Razor sat obediently by Danny's feet. He had walked close to us all the way back without a lead, which to me was also really impressive.

The number on their front door was 111. It looked like three people standing in a row.

A family.

When we got inside, I started to take my shoes off by the door.

'Don't bother,' said Danny, throwing his jacket on the floor by their phone.

The flat was really warm and had that kind

of pet shop smell. Clean, but animally.

Danny poured us some lemonade, and he took me to his room.

It was like Aladdin's cave. Two of the walls were lined with standing bookshelves and each of the shelves was full of books and trinkets and little models. The window was small and the books on the windowsill made it seem even smaller.

It's safe to say that if you had given me a piece of paper and a pencil and asked me to sketch what I thought Danny Jones's bedroom looked like before I'd seen it, my picture would've looked pretty different from the reality in front of me.

He had the same Spider-Man duvet cover as Dominic. I imagined Dom's face if I told him he shared duvet-cover taste with Danny Jones and smiled to myself. On the wall above his pillow I saw the list of places he wanted to visit.

PLACES TO GO
1. AUSTRALIAN OUTBACK
2. ALASKA
3. THE SERENGETI
4. SÃO PAULO
5. GIANT'S CAUSEWAY

'This is a cool room,' I said, sipping my lemonade.

Danny was busy pulling some heavy-looking books down from a high shelf.

'I wish it was bigger,' he said sitting on the floor. 'Check these out.'

They were thick leather-bound editions of some

old-school encyclopedias, the letters embossed on to the spines. He handed me one, and it was so heavy I thought my wrist might snap.

'I've read them all,' Danny said, opening one up in his lap. 'They were my dad's.'

The word 'dad' hung in the air between us. I wondered if Danny knew any more about his dad leaving than I knew about mine. Did he have to fight to keep his dad's stuff from the charity shop? Whatever had happened since, it was clear that Danny's dad hadn't been forgotten.

Before I knew what I was doing, the words jumped out of my mouth.

'Do you miss him?'

There was this moment of nothing, then Danny's face hardened. 'No,' he said. 'Good riddance.'

I opened the volume in my lap and pretended to read. Turned out Danny Jones wasn't a very good liar.

'I wonder where he's going next,' he said, looking at me.

I shrugged.

'Your dad? The letter?' said Danny.

'Oh,' I said. 'Yeah. Postman should've been by now. I'll find out when I get home.'

Danny's face lit up and he closed the book in his lap.

'We could go to yours now and find out?'

I squirmed. 'Better not. My mum has a nap cos she's on nights and my sister will only give us grief.'

Danny gave a nod, hiding his disappointment.

I watched his eyes move to the list above his pillow.

'That must be the coolest job in the world. Travelling for a reason,' he said.

'Yeah. I guess so.'

He stroked the old cover of his book. 'Remember that time you brought one of your dad's books in for show-and-tell? Was it Year Two?'

I tried to think.

'It was so cool,' he said. 'Somebody in your family, an actual writer.'

I had no idea what to say. I couldn't believe he remembered that far back.

'Thanks, Jay.' He looked at me, with the most genuine smile I think I'd ever seen. 'For letting me help.'

And something cold tapped my shoulder, like before, right by my neck. I touched where I'd felt it and there was nothing, then I felt it on the other side.

'You OK?' asked Danny.

'Yeah. I'm fine.'

But I wasn't. I didn't feel fine at all.

Then we heard the front door and Danny's face flooded with fear.

'Stay here,' he said in a serious voice. 'Whatever happens, don't come out.'

Then he left me, pulling his bedroom door firmly closed behind him.

⊕
⊛

Have you ever been at a friend's house while they're getting told off by their mum or dad?

It's awkward, right?

You feel bad for your friend, but maybe you also understand why they're in trouble and want to show the grown-up that you understand through your facial expressions.

Quite often their mum or dad will say something to you like, 'I'm sorry you have to see this, but he has to understand that he can't speak to me like that.'

Or maybe, 'Look at how you're embarrassing us in front of your friend.'

It's pretty tense, in my experience, but always feels under control, at least, because there's a parent involved.

What happened at Danny Jones's flat that afternoon felt very different. First off, I couldn't see what was happening, which made it worse. His bedroom door was closed and I heard him walking towards the kitchen. Cupboards and drawers slammed. Then I heard a man's voice. A kind of muffled barking. Then Danny said something. Then there was a thud. Like a stack of encyclopedias hitting the floor.

I thought about how much more dramatic everything seems through a wall. What you imagine is happening is always way worse, but this felt bad. Sometimes you can feel danger in the air, I truly believe that, and right then I definitely felt it.

I wanted to go and see what had happened, but the fear in Danny's face when he'd left the room kept me stuck to his bed. Then I heard footsteps stomping towards his room. Whoever had come back was heading this way. I was about to hide under his bed when I heard Danny's muffled voice from the other room and the footsteps stopped, turned and walked away. There was a little back-and-forth talking, more footsteps, then the front door opened and closed.

Every part of me wanted to leave. To run back home. But I didn't move. I just sat on Danny's bed and waited. Through the little window I could see the sky turning dark.

After what felt like ages, his bedroom door slowly opened, and Danny came in. His head was down and he was holding the side of his face.

'Are you OK?' I said, knowing it was a stupid question.

Danny started to put the encyclopedias away. 'I'm fine,' he said. 'Whoever made big brothers is an idiot.'

I could see his face was red on one cheek. I thought about Donna wrestling me into submission holds and pinning me down while she watched whole TV shows, and I got a sudden urge for her to walk into Danny's room right now.

'You should put some ice on it,' I said. 'My mum showed me how to make an ice pack.'

Danny gave me the most gentle smile. 'My mum showed me too.'

He pushed the last encyclopedia back on to the shelf and sat down next to me on the bed.

'Sometimes,' he said. 'Sometimes, I miss him.'

I wanted to put my arm around him. I wanted to pull him in for a hug to make him feel better, but somehow I could tell that I shouldn't. Him sitting down next to me was as much as he wanted. So instead I just sat quietly, next to Danny Jones, in a bedroom that nobody else would believe.

Week Three

26

How often do you think you lie?

Once a day? A couple of times a week? Never?

There are some people who'd answer that question with: 'I never tell lies, I'm an honest person.'

And maybe they believe that. Maybe it's actually true. But, like with most things, there are different levels with lying. Different sizes and reasons that make some things that aren't true feel different to others.

A university study done a few years ago estimated that the average human being lies approximately seven times a day. Seven.

Does that seem like a lot to you? Not much?

Whatever your response, I'm pretty sure I know one you tell quite regularly.

1.

How are you?

Fine.

Is the 'fine' part a lie? I'm sure sometimes you are feeling fine and the answer is true, but how many times has someone asked you how you are, and you've actually been feeling pretty rubbish, but still said 'fine'? I'm guessing at least a few. Maybe you didn't want the person to worry, or maybe you just didn't feel like talking much, but if you answered 'fine' and didn't mean it, does the 'fine' become a lie?

Does that count?

How about this one?

2.

Check out my new shoes! I got them for my birthday – do you like them?

Yeah. They're great. Really great.

You don't think they're great at all. You think

they're some of the ugliest shoes you've ever seen, or at least just pretty boring. But you didn't say that, did you? You said they were great, because you didn't want to hurt the person's feelings. Because you didn't want to start an argument. So is 'They're great' a lie? Maybe you mean they're great for them. The shoes aren't to your taste, but you respect the fact that the person loves them.

You see my point? It can get complicated and muddy, and these examples are only answers to simple questions. Imagine how muddy things can get when it's you making up the whole thing to start with.

Trust me. It's mud city.

27

To be honest, Week Three is a bit of a blur.

I carried on making things up. Danny went to work on a new report about São Paulo. When I gave him the letter and he realized it was a location from his dream list, he almost exploded with excitement.

At school I genuinely felt like a completely new person. Everything had changed. Everyone looked at me differently. People I'd hardly spoken to my whole time in the juniors were coming up to me, asking about Dad and other things I'd made up.

I'd gone from feeling like it was just me and Dominic, to it seeming like almost everyone at school wanted to be my friend. Me. Jason Gardner. The cool kid.

Dominic was getting pretty agitated about my

lack of commitment to Full Force. His rehearsal timetable hadn't really worked and after the awkward dinner with his mum and dad, I'd been avoiding going over there even more.

Walking home together on Friday of that week I could feel the weight of Danny's São Paulo report in my bag. It was almost encyclopedia-thick and must've taken him hours to make. I thought about the look on his face as he'd handed it over to me at lunch, and felt the cold tapping on my shoulder again. I started running through the weeks' stories, trying to ignore it as Dom rambled on about dance power moves and floor work.

Then, as we reached Mr Rogers's corner shop, he whacked my arm.

'Oi! What was that for?'

Our following conversation went roughly like this:

Dom: You're not listening!

Me: What?

Dom: See. I knew it!

Me: Yes, I am.

Dom: So, what did I just say then, if you're listening?

Me: Don't you remember yourself?

Dom: Answer the question.

Me: I don't know, something about the moon?

Dom: I knew it! Why don't you listen any more?

Me: I *am* listening.

Dom: No, you're too busy thinking about your stupid stories.

Me: What? Shut up! They're not stupid!

Dom: They're not real.

Me: Dom, I'm just a bit tired.

Dom: From what? Not from practising, I know that much.

Me: Leave it, will you?

Dom: We need to practise! We only have three weeks left and we've done nothing. The routine has to be super sharp if we're going to win the talent show.

Me: We're not going to win any talent show.

Dom: Not if we don't practise!

He was waving his arms around like a football manager on the sidelines. I felt my head dropping. I was really tired. Maintaining my cool was taking almost all my brain capacity, and the last thing I needed was Dominic trying to fill my head with the stupid talent show. I sat down on the low brick wall outside the shop we'd walked past for years, and I guess I must've looked troubled, because out of nowhere, Dominic apologized.

'I'm sorry, man,' he said, sitting down next to me.

I looked at the little note I'd made on the back of my hand with biro:

Mr Benn. £2m. Cheque.

At afternoon break, I'd told Tracey and Rupinder from the other Year 6 class that my next-door neighbour, old Mr Benn, had won the lottery. When they asked me how much, I said I didn't know exact figures, but that I'd seen him outside his house holding a big cheque, posing for photographs.

Another little bag of details to add to my already covered wall.

'You wanna talk about it?' said Dom.

I looked at him.

He shrugged. 'Mum said I should ask.'

Even when he didn't need to, Dom couldn't help but tell the truth.

'What else did she say?' I asked.

'She said that, when something bad happens, people can behave differently. Funny. She said that's how we deal with something we don't like.'

'I see.'

Dom pulled an uncomfortable expression. 'Like someone leaving.'

I looked down.

'She said a good friend would ask if the person wanted to talk about it.' He nudged my shoulder with his. 'I want to be a good friend.'

'You are a good friend,' I said, looking up again.

'It doesn't feel like it lately,' he said, scraping the ground with his foot. 'Lately it seems like you're more bothered about everyone else.'

'Dom, look –' and I was about to say something real. Something true. I swear I was. Something that would make him feel closer to me. Sitting right next to my oldest friend, I really wanted to, but before I could, Dom said:

'I just think it'd be a good thing to do, you know? Help you feel better. I really think we could win.'

And just like that, the moment had gone. The space between us felt wider than ever and I just wanted to go home.

'I need to get back,' I said.

'What about rehearsals?'

'Sorry. Mum's taking me to Merry Hill, for new trainers. It's her only day off.'

Just like that. A complete lie. Easy as breathing. To my oldest friend. Mum wasn't taking me to Merry Hill. She didn't have a day off, and nobody had even mentioned new trainers. I'd just made it up so I wouldn't have to go to his house and feel awkward with his happy mum and dad, and pretend to be excited about the completely awful idea that was Full Force.

A BIT ABOUT LYING

There are things that the human body does when it's telling a lie, right?

Little 'reveals' that, if you can spot them, give away when someone is not telling the truth.

How many can you think of?

I'm not sure how much experience you have already, but just in case you're new to this, here's a list of things to look out for to spot when someone may be lying.

- **Eye contact.** Bit obvious, you're probably thinking. You have to look someone in the eye for them to believe you, everyone knows that. But it's a bit more complicated if you want to spot someone who isn't a Level One

183

amateur. You want to look for an amount that feels unnatural. Not enough, and someone is worried about you looking into them and seeing the lie. Too much, and someone is trying to bluff and convince you that what they are saying is the most true thing ever. Inexperienced liars will often stare at you way too intensely as they speak, like an owl.

• **Smiling.** Of course, it depends on the subject, but again it's all about what feels natural. Someone who speaks without any emotion in their facial expression may be worried that their feelings will betray them. They think the truth is neutral. It isn't. The truth always comes with emotion attached. On the flip side, someone who is grinning the whole time, trying too hard to appear friendly, is quite often a slimy salesperson, trying to make you buy something you don't really want. In this case, a lie.

• **Sweating.** This might sound a little basic, but it's surprising how hot lying can make you. Blood temperature has been scientifically proven to rise when telling a lie. Sweat usually begins at the side of the head at the temples, and on the top lip. Slightly more experienced liars have been known to use handkerchiefs to mop their faces when talking.

• **Touching the face or head.** When a person lies, their body sometimes tries to get involved to help. If someone touches their face as they speak, it is often because they are unconsciously trying to hide from their own guilt. Often a liar will touch or scratch one of their ear lobes in a fake display of feeling relaxed. If this action is repeated, it's an even clearer sign.

OK, that's all Level One stuff. You probably knew all those ones already. Let's crank it up a notch. Here's a couple of Level Two ones.

We'll use the scenario of 'The Last Biscuit'.

Basically, someone took the last biscuit, and you want to know if it's the person you suspect, so you ask:

'Did you take the last biscuit?'

And here's the response you get:

'No! I did *not* take the last biscuit! I resent the fact that you would ask me that! I'm so offended that I can't even stand to be in the same room as you right now! I'm leaving! Aaaaarghhh!'

And the person storms out.

How do you know that is a lie?

• **Too much emotion.** In an attempt to distract you, the person has pumped too much emotion into their words in the hope that you might even feel guilty for asking them, and go on to your next possible suspect.

Let's try another. Same scenario, so same question: 'Did you take the last biscuit?'

This time, the response you get is:

'Me? **No I didn't take the last biscuit, I do love biscuits, though, I can still remember my first ever biscuit, I was three, or maybe even two, it was with my granny and I was sitting on her knee and she gave me a Jammie Dodger and I took a bite and I was like, "Oooohh, this is amazing," and then she showed me custard creams and bourbons and Jaffa Cakes, and I love, love, love biscuits and, no, I didn't take the last biscuit, nope, not me, not at all, no way, OK, bye.'**

How do you know that is a lie?

• **Too much information.** Again, in an attempt to distract you, the person has packed in so much information that you become swept up in their little story, maybe picturing them on their grandma's knee or even thinking about your own grandma and remembering happy times from when you were little, thus completely losing a sense of what you were even asking them in the first place.

You see? It's a tricky business.

Now, most people don't get beyond that, but there are some who are even more sneaky.

When you start getting into the realm of Level Three and beyond, it really is a minefield. But those people do exist. There are people in the world who have crafted the skill of lying to a level where it's almost impossible to tell.

What do you know about micro-gestures?

Do you know what a gesture is?

gesture *(noun)*
An expressive movement or action.

Not to be confused with:

jester *(noun)*

A person with pointy shoes who shakes a stick with bells on and falls over to make the king and queen laugh in medieval times.

Examples of gestures:

1. Waving = 'Hello' or 'Goodbye'.

2. Thumbs up = 'That is good.'

3. Thumbs down = 'That is not good.'

4. Pinching nose with one hand while waving the other hand in front of face = 'That stinks.'

Well, as you might guess, micro-gestures are the same, only way smaller.

A blink. A millisecond glance up and to the left. Half a cough before the important word. A twitch at the corner of the mouth. Tiny, tiny movements that most eyes can't even see, but they're there.

A very wise man told me early on, 'Every lie is dirty. None of them are clean. It's just that some are neater than others. And some are messy from the start.'

Try it in the mirror.

Go to your nearest bathroom. Bring this book with you.

Right, now stare at your own reflection and say something that isn't true:

'I just won fourteen million pounds.'

'I can run faster than a cheetah.'

Anything? Did you seem natural? Not too much or too little emotion?

Try something nearer to the truth.

'I am the most popular person in school.'

'I have never been scared of spiders.'

'I never, ever, ever get annoyed with my parents.'

Look at yourself. Do you believe you? Were there any little tics that gave you away?

It's easier in the mirror too. Imagine a room full of eyes on you as you say it. What that feels like.

See, the thing is . . . What I've learned, and what I truly believe, is that our bodies are honest.

My body. Your body. Everybody's body.

They don't want to lie. No matter what our minds might hope when they hatch their sneaky plans, our bodies don't really want any part of it. That's why they twitch. That's why the corner of our mouth moves in a weird way. Or our eyebrows slide a few millimetres to the side. Our bodies don't want to lie. They don't even want to be anywhere near a lie. So when when we tell a lie, or we're faced with a lie and don't call it out, point a finger or walk off, a little part of our body tries to run away.

29

Sometimes my dreams are just full memories, playing out like films as I sleep . . .

Me in the car, sitting in the back seat, Donna across from me, Dad driving, Mum next to him. I'm watching the grey concrete buildings of the city slide past us as we drive. The morning sun is intense. There's music on the radio. The car feels light.

We don't know where we're headed, because we're on one of Dad's spontaneous road trips. Just an hour ago we were all sitting in the living room, eating cereal, watching Saturday morning cartoons. Then Dad suddenly stood up like someone shot electricity through the seat of his chair. 'Everyone, get dressed!'

Next thing, we're in the car, on our way to who knows where.

One song turns into two songs, then three songs and a whole album, as the grey concrete starts to spread out and buildings become less and less. After a while everything is different shades of green, and there are fields dotted with cows and the sky feels bigger and full of possibility. I can feel a crackle in my stomach, the excitement of the unknown.

Without warning, Dad pulls over next to a row of thick privet hedges. There's nothing obviously special about this spot, but Dad seems sure. 'Everybody out!' he says, and opens his door.

The glare of the sun makes me squint as we all get out and stand next to the car.

'What are we doing?' asks Donna.

Dad answers with a smile, then walks straight into the hedge and disappears.

I look at Donna; Donna looks at Mum; Mum looks at us both, and shrugs.

The hedge has rough twigs that scratch my arms as we squeeze through. Donna is starting to moan as we burrow through the shady tunnel.

I can smell the soil. Then the light hits us again and we're out, standing at the edge of a huge field, ploughed into straight, brown, earthy rows. There's a white farmhouse in the distance and, right in the middle of the field, about fifty metres away from us, is Dad, talking to a man in a straw hat. He turns to us and waves us over. The other man just stands there, his arms stretched out either side of him.

It's a scarecrow.

As the three of us reach Dad, I can see the sack for a head, with eyes and a mouth painted on. Its chequered shirt is weather-beaten, and the pockets of its dungarees have straw sticking out of them.

'What's going on, Dad?' says Donna, shielding her eyes from the sun.

Dad points at the scarecrow. 'This is Greg. Greg, meet everyone.'

Greg doesn't move. Dad waves. 'Say hello, everyone.'

'I'm not saying hello to a scarecrow,' says Donna, looking at Mum.

Dad looks at me. I wave. 'Hi, Greg.'

Donna rolls her eyes. Mum looks at Dad. Dad shrugs. 'Guess he's not her type.' Mum looks stern, then cracks a smile, and the pair of them laugh. Donna doesn't.

'This is ridiculous,' she says. 'Why are we even here?'

Dad holds out his hands like he's offering her a gift. 'It's a story. This will be the time you turned down a date from a scarecrow.'

He waits for Donna to take his hands. She doesn't.

'Jesus, Dad. Are you serious? Not everything has to be a story!' Then

she turns and walks back towards the hedge. Dad looks at Mum. Mum shrugs, then walks after Donna.

I watch the pair of them getting smaller. Dad turns to me.

'Just me and you then, big man.' There's a sadness in his smile.

I point at the scarecrow. 'And Greg.'

Then Dad hugs me, his heavy arms squeezing, and it feels amazing and safe, and I just want to sleep right here. In his arms.

❀
❀

I woke up needing to wee.

I don't know about you, but whenever I do that, there's always that first moment when you don't want to get up. Your dream still has you in its arms all cosy in bed and the idea of getting out from under your duvet is the worst, and the long trip to the bathroom feels like an Arctic expedition.

My next thought (and I'm not that proud to

admit this) is always, What if I just weed right here? What If I just lay back, relaxed my bladder and let it go? How bad would that really be? Wee is pretty warm. It might feel quite nice. I think I'm gonna do it.

Then comes the flash forward to feeling guilty and having to go into your mum's room and tell her what happened and the painful minutes of standing there in shame as she changes your sheets and tips up your mattress.

So, I got up.

My eyes adjusted to the dark as I walked to the bathroom. I left the light off, and everything looked like an old black-and-white film. The moonlight through the bathroom window caught in the tap water as I quietly washed my hands. When I came back out on to the landing, I noticed a stick of light on the carpet further down the landing. Donna's light was still on. She pretty much went to bed when she liked, so it wasn't weird for her to be up late, but this felt really late, even for her.

I edged closer to her door, curious. Mum's bedroom door was shut and lifeless.

I got right up to Donna's and put my naked toes in the line of light. I couldn't hear anything from inside. I could probably count the times I've been allowed into Donna's room in my whole life on one hand. Usually she'd give me a dead arm for even looking at her door, but there's something about the middle of the night that changes the rules, right? Have you experienced that? Like when you're on a trip somewhere and you get home really late, everything feels different? Things that aren't allowed in the day are now possible. A sneaky hot chocolate. A delicate question. The middle of the night loves risks.

So I tapped. Gently, of course, but she heard me, and the next thing I knew, her door was opening.

30

I sat in the chair at her desk. Donna was sitting on her bed, legs crossed, an open red shoebox with folded papers inside next to her. Bruce Lee was doing a high kick on the wall next to the wardrobe. Donna's bedside lamp made all her music posters cast little jagged shadows at their corners.

'Bad dream?' she said. And in a strange coincidence, right then, my eyes fell on the photograph next to her bed of all four of us standing outside a caravan holding ice creams. I looked about five, grinning at my two-scoop cone. Donna was licking her lolly trying to seem cool while Mum and Dad had tangled their arms together so they were licking each other's ice creams. I had no idea who took the picture, but as Donna looked at me, I stared at Dad. He only existed in photographs and dreams now.

'It's OK,' said Donna. 'I've been having them too.'

'You have?'

I must've sounded a little bit too shocked because Donna's voice changed to offended.

'Yes, Jason. I am also a human being.'

We laughed a little bit, then stopped. I still couldn't believe where I was sitting. Donna put some paper back into the shoebox and closed the lid.

'Ask what you want,' she said. And my chair felt warm. Like I was sitting in a spotlight on some kind of game show where I'm supposed to know loads about something, but my brain is drawing a complete blank. Donna was talking to me. Like a regular person. I wondered if that was how it worked: when someone leaves, does their role get filled by the people who are still there?

'Why did he go?' I said.

There was a pause. I watched Donna chew a couple of possible answers and swallow them.

Then she did the best impression of Mum sighing I've ever seen, and said:

'Because he wanted to.'

I felt my throat getting tight, the ticking in my stomach start, and something tapping my shoulder all at the same time.

'Did we do something wrong? Was it me?'

'No!' She shuffled down the bed a bit towards me. 'People make choices, Jay.'

I got up before she could say more. I felt like I was going to cry, and I didn't need to hear the same script again. Donna jumped up and cut me off before I could get to her door.

'Hey. Wait up.'

She leaned down so her face was near mine. I could smell her peach shampoo.

I looked everywhere except right at her.

'Oi,' she said, holding my shoulders. My face was doing the tingly thing it does right before I'm going to cry. I didn't want her to see me cry. I know it sounds stupid. I wanted her to think I was strong like she was, but I could feel the tears coming.

'Can I show you something?' said Donna.

And my surprise stopped my eyes from leaking, just in time.

She led me to her bed and sat me down.

'Some things don't make any sense. No matter how much you want them to.'

She picked up the shoebox and handed it to me. 'Have a look.'

I held it in my lap.

'Open it,' she said.

So I did.

It was full of little notes. Torn pieces of paper with handwritten scribbles in different-coloured pens. Quotes and doodles. I saw a badly drawn unicorn and what looked like a man bending over farting lightning.

'I kept them all,' she said sheepishly. 'Every single idea we scribbled together from when I was little. All our stupid stories.'

I touched the notes at the top. Some of them had coloured glitter sprinkled at the edges.

I couldn't read the words clearly, but I

recognized some of the handwriting as Dad's.

I looked at Donna. My big sister. Strongest fifteen-year-old around. She smiled and shrugged.

'I don't understand it either.'

Week Four

31

Dear Jason,

The São Paulo report was excellent. Please give an extra special thanks to Danny. My time here has been very productive. My next destination is New York. I have meetings with the publishers to discuss my progress. I look forward to your helpful research.

Dad

32

Do you ever feel like your body is here, but your mind is somewhere completely different? Like your mind got up, put on its comfiest shoes, opened a door at the back of your head, waved goodbye to your body and walked off towards the sunset?

I do. I get it a lot.

And it happened to me that Monday morning.

School was winding down, with only two weeks before we broke up for summer and said goodbye to the building forever. Mr Bukowski didn't even ask to see our homework, which was lucky because I'd completely forgotten all about it. I'd spent the weekend watching films with Donna and going over the notes on my ever-filling wall.

The energy in class felt kind of lazy, and I was

glad because it meant not many people asked me about Dad or anything else. At the end of the week we were due to get our final reports, but the general feeling was that nobody really cared since we wouldn't be coming back after summer anyway.

Dominic wasn't talking much. He'd been quiet on the walk into school that morning too, but I was fine with it because it meant I didn't have to listen to him moaning about our stupid Full Force rehearsals. Him being quiet was fine with me.

People were making posters to put up around the school to advertise the show to parents and, as lessons went on around me, my body clicked into autopilot and my mind packed a lunchbox, grabbed some bus fare and said 'See you later'.

This is where it went . . .

❂

Me, riding a horse. A big horse. Only it's not really a horse. It's Gus. A horse-sized version of Gus. And I'm riding him, charging through the streets waving a sword like I'm some kind of medieval knight. But it's not actually a sword. It's a rolled-up piece of paper. A map. I'm riding a horse-sized Gus through town, waving a rolled-up map like a sword.

Then Gus stops too quickly and I'm flipped forward, off his back, over his head. I'm spinning through the air, still holding the rolled-up map and Gus is shouting something. In a big horse-dog voice, Gus is shouting, 'I'm sorry!' And I'm spinning through the air and I'm shouting too. I'm upside down, shouting, 'I'm sorry!' And then I hit the floor. I splat on the pavement and somehow the map has rolled itself out. The map is rolled out flat on the pavement and I'm lying flat on top of it and my whole body is aching from hitting the concrete and I'm groaning, 'I'm sorry,' and I look up and there's people standing all around me. A crowd circling me and the map, and I see Danny. And Dominic. And another Danny and another Dominic and everyone is either Danny or Dominic and they're all looking down at me and pointing and shaking their heads, and I'm groaning and then I notice they're not pointing at me, they're pointing at the map. It's covered in scribbles. Black circles and rushed notes. And my whole body aches and I'm surrounded and one of the Dannys says . . .

'Are you OK?'

I blinked and I was standing in the cloakroom, Danny Jones next to me.

It was morning break.

'Are you OK?' said Danny again. I rubbed my eyes, trying to get my bearings.

OK? I wasn't sure what I felt, but OK wasn't it.

'Yeah,' I said. 'Bit tired.'

Danny just stood there. Looking at my bag on the peg. He was waiting for Dad's latest letter. As I took it out, I noticed Dominic standing over by the toilets, watching us.

I felt the spike of guilt in my stomach as I handed over the fake letter to Danny.

'New York? Sick!' Danny's face was full of excitement. 'I knew he'd like the São Paulo one.

Your dad is the coolest, Jay!'

He started to walk off. Dad? Why was Dad the coolest? I was the one making this stuff up.

'You coming?' said Danny, turning back. 'We need to get started on this.'

He held up the letter. Dad didn't write that, Danny, I thought to myself. I'm the cool one.

I looked over at Dominic. His face told me that he wanted to talk.

I didn't have time for Full Force. I had enough on my plate with trying to juggle everything I'd made up, and being with Danny. The letters meant so much to him, I couldn't drop the ball now, or he'd be gutted.

'Come on!' Danny was holding the hall door open for me.

I looked at him, then back at Dom. I knew I was letting him down. It felt like my body was split in two halves, and the halves were wrestling each other. Dom smiled his crooked smile. And I wanted to smile back, but I didn't.

'Jay! The report!' Danny was getting impatient.

He was eager to be part of Dad's cool.

I looked at Dominic again, shrugged, then followed Danny through the door.

Out of order, right? That's what you're thinking. I get it.

How could I do that? Abandon my oldest friend?

I could make up an excuse. I could try and make you see it how I did at the time, but the truth of it is, right then, I didn't even feel in control of what I was doing.

It felt like I'd got on to a roller coaster and couldn't see how to get off.

guilt *(noun)*
A bad feeling caused by knowing or thinking that you have done something bad or wrong.

33

The next morning, while Donna was upstairs in the shower, I sat with my Rice Krispies at the table, making notes about a story I'd told some Year 4s the day before, about a time I got my hand stuck in the grate at the bottom of the swimming pool and managed to hold my breath for nearly two full minutes. They had lots of questions and I knew they'd pester me for more details. As I jotted down ideas and tested myself, Mum came home from her night shift at the hospital.

'Morning, sweetheart,' she said, dropping her bag and sitting down opposite me.

I smiled and carried on with my notes. Incredible Hulk trunks. Old lifeguard with walrus moustache.

Mum pulled a biro out of her hair. 'You look

tired,' she said. 'Did you sleep OK?'

'Yeah,' I lied. Truth was, I had been up until after midnight checking details and rehearsing stories besides this one. Truth was, I felt exhausted. But at this point, the truth didn't feel like an option.

'What you working on?' Mum said, pointing at my notes.

I folded up my paper and put my bowl on top of it. 'Nothing. Just a thing for school. We're writing stories.'

I watched her face change as I said the words. Mentioning stories put Dad in the room.

I wanted to say something to make it better, but weirdly, nothing came. I opened my mouth, but it was like something was blocking the words, so I just ate another spoonful.

'I'm sorry, love,' said Mum, looking at me with her kind super-boss nurse eyes. 'I know it's been hard. And I know I've been working lots.'

I just sat and chewed. Mum slipped off her shoes and started rubbing her feet.

'It's complicated,' she said. 'Your dad's a complicated man.'

It almost felt like she was defending him.

'Everybody's complicated,' I said, and I couldn't hide the frustration in my voice.

Mum felt it.

'That's very true, Jay.'

She rested her chin in her palm.

'That's it?' I said. 'That's all you're gonna say?'

I took another spoonful and felt the ticking in my stomach, only this time it was different somehow, more spiky. I could see Mum fighting her emotions back. She did the thing where she brushes hair behind her ear and folds her arms.

'I'm afraid that's all I really know. I don't have the answers, love. I wish I did.'

And I believed her. She really didn't understand either. Just like Donna. Just like me.

I nodded my kindest nod, grabbed my bowl, and the letter, and stood up. I hadn't got any more real information about Dad. But it felt like me and Mum had shared something.

'How was your cake-eating contest?' said Mum.

'What?'

'Frances told me the plan last week. Dom's birthday.'

And it felt like someone had punched me in the chest.

Dom's birthday.

Today was the 10th, which meant Dominic's birthday was yesterday. And I'd completely forgotten! I felt my legs wobble, and leaned on the back of the chair to steady myself. That's why he was so quiet walking into school yesterday! And in class! That's why he wanted to speak to me. Not Full Force or Dad's mission. And I'd brushed him off like it wasn't important. He must think I don't care about his birthday at all!

'Are you OK, love?' said Mum.

Every year we did something together on our birthdays. Paintballing. Treasure hunt in the woods. Cake-eating contest. And I'd forgotten.

Because of
everything
else. Because of Dad.

'Sweetheart?'

I looked at Mum. Get yourself together, I told myself. You're cool, remember?

So be cool.

'I'm fine,' I said. 'Think I just stood up too quickly. I better go, I'll be late for school.'

On my walk towards Mr Rogers's corner shop, I tried to come up with a story for Dom. Something to explain why I could've possibly forgotten my oldest friend's birthday. Something that could have happened at home. It would have to be something big. Something dramatic that would switch my guilt into his sympathy.

But Dom wasn't there.

I checked my watch. 8.45 a.m. Same time as always. Same time every morning since they started letting us walk to school by ourselves.

I looked back down the road. Nothing.

I checked my watch again. 8.46. 8.47.

A cool breeze whipped around me. 8.48. Where was he?

I waited until 8.55 before I left.

By the time I got to school, the bell had long gone. I walked into reception and made up a story about taking the bin out, locking myself out and having to wait for my mum.

When I walked into class, Dominic was there. Sitting in his seat, normal as you like.

I waited for him to look my way, but he didn't.

'Nice of you to join us,' said Mr Bukowski in his crazily calm voice. Danny Jones smiled at me from his seat, no doubt already hours into his New York research assignment.

'Sorry, sir,' I said, and my voice felt small.

I felt everyone's eyes on me as I walked to my chair.

Everyone's, that is, except my oldest friend.

34

The rest of the week passed by in a kind of daze.

More stories.

More late nights.

More tiredness.

I walked into school and back home by myself. Dominic was avoiding me like I had the plague and I'd started to notice something. A feeling. At the back of my mind. Almost like a noise. Like one long constant violin note, playing the whole time, making it almost impossible to relax.

It's a weird thing, being seen as cool. Being popular. In a way it's almost like a job. You have to work to keep it going. Do the things you're supposed to do, say the things you're supposed to say. It's like you're spending your whole day carrying a pretend version of yourself that you can't put down until you get home, and when you do put it down, instead of getting to actually enjoy all the attention, all you want to do is pass out.

My head was full. My wall was full. Everything was full. So full that, to be honest – and this might sound crazy – I wasn't even thinking about Dad.

There really wasn't room.

❀

That Friday afternoon, as we packed our bags at the end of the day, I had this moment. Holding Danny Jones's New York report in my hands, I looked around the room. Everything felt so different. It was like I was wearing a costume that looked exactly like me, but felt somehow detached.

I looked at Danny's hand-drawn picture of the Empire State Building on the cover:

I looked over at Danny as he was zipping up his pencil case, and a thought hit me.

The old Danny Jones, class bully, who'd filled us with so much dread, was gone. A whole character erased from the story of our lives and replaced with a new one. A busy, excited reporter, learning about the world and helping a travelling writer write the best story ever. A friend.

I looked at Dom as he neatly folded up his jacket and slid it into his bag. He felt far away, let down by me: his failed dance partner, forgetter of his birthday, busy in my own world. As we started to leave, I almost said his name. I felt it in my throat but, just as I stepped out of the room, Mr Bukowski asked to speak to me.

35

'Have a seat,' he said, and his crazily calm voice felt weird in the empty classroom.

Out through the window I could see crowds of people crossing the playground. Everybody was heading off for the weekend.

I sat down in the chair next to his desk. Mr Bukowski just sat across from me, a wide smile on his shaven-bear face. I wasn't sure whether I was supposed to say something. It seemed like he was waiting for me to.

'Sir?'

He just kept smiling. And the ticking in my stomach felt like it had back on the first day after half-term, when everything started. With the book report. I was nervous.

Mr Bukowski leaned forward on his desk. 'How are you?'

And it was like his voice passed right through me. Like I could feel it in my bones.

I shuffled uncomfortably in my seat.

'Me? I'm fine, sir. Yeah. Fine. Why?'

'Fine?' said Mr Bukowski, nodding slowly. 'I see.'

What was going on? It somehow felt like an interrogation without any actual interrogating. My hands were shaking. I sat on them to keep them still.

Mr Bukowski stood up and walked to the window.

'One week left,' he said, staring out on to the playground. 'Then it's all over.'

All over? That felt ominous. What did he mean? School? Everything?

It felt a bit like a scene from a film. A scene where something important is revealed.

'I've been speaking to Dominic,' he said, turning to face me, and I felt myself starting to sweat. Dominic? What had Dominic said? Had Dominic told him what I was doing? Had Dominic told him the truth?

'Dominic, sir?' I faked confusion.

Mr Bukowski walked back to his desk and sat

on the edge, hands in his lap, eyes on me.

'Yes. We couldn't help but notice how popular you've become recently.'

I was really squirming now. He knew. I knew he knew, but his face wasn't revealing anything.

'Particularly with Danny Jones,' he said, allowing one eyebrow to rise slightly. My nervous mouth went into overdrive.

'Danny, sir? No, not really. I mean, we've been working on something together. It's a kind of . . . project, sir. Danny's been helping me, yeah, a story project. You're going to love it, sir. It's really something, but, no . . . I mean, everything's fine, yeah, totally fine.'

My heart was kicking inside my chest like an angry bull trapped in a garden shed. I did my best to hold eye contact and seem natural.

Mr Bukowski didn't move. The air in the room felt like it was getting thinner. Like someone was sucking out the oxygen. Then he nodded.

'Stories, eh?'

He stroked the bottom of his beard. 'Well, as long as you know what you're doing.' He leaned forward until he was so close he could have reached me if he'd wanted to.

'You know what you're doing, right?'

I forced my bone-dry throat to swallow. 'Yes, sir.'

A pause. Him sitting still on the edge of his desk; me caught in the tractor beam of his stare. Then he clapped his hands.

'Have a good weekend then,' he said, and started tidying up his desk.

I waited for a moment, to compose myself, then stood up. And left.

❧

Walking home by myself, I couldn't get his words out of my head.

As long as you know what you're doing . . . As long as you know what you're doing.

It was like a line from a song that wouldn't leave my skull.

As long as you know what you're doing.

Of course I knew what I was doing. I was doing what Dad did. I was making up stories. I was being cool. Yes, I was tired, but that was the sacrifice I had to make. Yes, my oldest friend was upset with me, but you can't build something important without making sacrifices.

Mr Bukowski wouldn't understand that, like Dominic didn't, but that wasn't my fault.

Like most important things, cool comes at a cost. I said the words out loud: 'Cool comes at a cost. Just ask Dad.'

Those words surprised me.

I caught my reflection in the glass of the empty bus stop and stopped walking. I tried to picture Dad there, standing behind me. Two cool people, who understand how things work. But I couldn't. All I saw was me.

I still looked like me, no matter how different things felt.

'I know what I'm doing.' I watched my reflection mouth the words as I said them again: 'I know what I'm doing.'

And I did. I knew.

Deep down in my stomach. I knew all too well.

36

Next morning was Saturday and I was ready for a lie-in. A morning cut off from the world, curled up safely under my duvet, was exactly what I needed.

When Mum walked into my room at half past eight that morning, it was clear that she had other ideas.

'Come on!' she said, leaning in through my open doorway. 'I need your help.'

I burrowed down further under my covers, hoping it might make me invisible. If it worked, then Mum must've had X-ray vision.

'Come on, sweetheart. I need a big strong boy to help me carry.'

I felt her weight as she sat down on the end of my bed.

'I'm still asleep,' I said, in my best still-asleep voice.

'Wow!' said Mum. 'You've been busy.'

I threw off my duvet and sat up. She was staring at the map. My wall covered in fragments of lies stories. I felt exposed.

'OK, I'm up,' I said, jumping out of bed. Gus was still asleep under my radiator. 'Where are we going?'

I started helping Mum up and walking her out of my room. Her eyes were still on my wall.

'Shopping,' she said. 'I thought you could help me cook.'

'Sounds great.' I eased her out of the door. 'Just give me a minute to get dressed. Can I smell toast? Mmm, I'd love some toast. Can you make me some toast please, Mum? For strength, right?'

Mum had this kind of dazed look on her face, like she was half lost in a memory. I touched her shoulder to snap her out of it.

'Mum? Toast? Strength? Shopping?'

'What? Oh, yeah. Toast. Strength. Good. I'll do it now.'

It took us fifteen minutes to finally find a space in the supermarket car park. A big, black van was wedged into the space on my side. My door banged it as I tried to get out.

'Whoops. I don't think I can fit, Mum . . . Mum?'

Mum was just staring out through the windscreen. An old man, carrying an orange shopping bag in each hand, shuffled past the front of the car. 'Mum? We're here.'

'It's all stories,' she said, in a soft, nurse-like voice.

I pulled my door closed. 'What?'

'He used to say, "It's all stories, Ange. We just follow where they lead us."'

Her expression seemed trapped between two places. I knew she meant Dad. And it felt like she could see him right there. Then she looked at me.

'He could be so full of it sometimes. He really could.'

The whole time since he'd left, this was the first negative thing I'd heard her say about him.

And I liked it. It felt like a completely new flavour after weeks of the same taste. And she wasn't finished.

'We don't have to live your dad's story, Jay,' she said, touching my shoulder. 'You understand me? We get to write our own.'

And it was genuinely the coolest line I'd ever heard. I felt myself smiling at her. Mum smiled back.

'Come on. You can get out my side.'

❧

The supermarket was like an old people's carnival. I steered the trolley as Mum checked her list. The plan was to make curry for two. Donna was staying at her friend Lucy's.

At the bottom of the vegetable aisle, we bumped into Frances, Dom's mum. I hadn't seen her since the awkward dinner, but I knew she must know I'd forgotten Dom's birthday. I felt so embarrassed as she gave me a sympathetic look.

'Look who it is!' she said, putting on a voice like a game-show host.

I felt Mum
freeze up a little
bit at the
possibility
of having to
talk about Dad,
but then
Frances
touched Mum's
arm and smiled and the cold
between them seemed to melt. They
clicked into old-friend-conversation mode,
which, as I'm sure you know, between mums in
the supermarket takes AGES. I was left standing
there like a pointless statue. I picked up a
pumpkin and held it like a shot-put, just for
something to do.

'Dominic's here somewhere,' said Frances,
breaking out of their conversation for a second.
'I think he's over there looking at comics.'

I looked at Mum, who nodded and waved me
off in the general direction of the magazines.

37

Dominic was sitting on the floor cross-legged, reading an *Amazing Spider-Man* like he was in his own living room or something, and didn't see me approaching. I took some heavy breaths to prep myself as I got closer. Outside of school felt like neutral ground for an apology and, right now, sitting quietly with him and  reading a comic felt like the best idea ever.

'Hey,' I said, looking down at him.

Dominic looked up, and his face went all cold. He didn't say anything back and I just stood there, in a puddle of awkward.

'What you reading?' I asked. Dom tilted the comic so I could see. Spider-Man was battling the Sinister Six.

'Cool.'

Still nothing back. A woman moved past us pushing a trolley full of bulging bags and two little crying girls. I waited till she was out of earshot, then I pointed. 'You think they had a two-for-one sale on crying babies?'

I forced a laugh, hoping Dom would join me. He didn't. The tension between us was clear.

'Not hanging out with your best friend then?' he said eventually, looking past me for someone.

'What? Who?'

'Danny Jones.' His voice was all sharp. Aiming to poke me.

'Danny Jones is not my best friend,' I said.

Dom screwed up his face. 'You could've fooled me.'

And even though I knew why he was annoyed, my defences kicked in and I couldn't stop myself biting back.

'Well, fooling you's not very hard to do, is it?'

Dom closed his comic and stood up. The two of us stood arm's length apart like we were about to fight.

'Well, maybe I'm the only one you haven't fooled, Mr Liar.'

I felt the word hit me in the stomach like a punch, my weight rocking back on my heels.

Mr Liar?

'I'm not a liar.'

'Yes you are. Mr Liar.'

Pain in my ribs.

'Yeah, well, why don't you just go and cry to Mr Bukowski?' I spat the words at him.

Dom looked confused. 'I didn't cry to Mr Bukowski.'

'You may as well have done. Snitch.'

'What are you talking about?'

'You're just jealous.'

'Of what? Being a liar?'

'Shut up!'

'No, you shut up!' He stepped forward as he

said it, and I honestly thought he was going to punch me. He didn't, of course. Dominic Clarke didn't punch people. Dominic Clarke was too good.

For a split second I felt the urge to just grab him and hug. To try and squeeze out all of the bad stuff that was making him angry with me. But I didn't.

Instead, for some reason, I pushed it further.

'No, Dom. You shut up. Still planning your little dance routine?' I mimed my worst octopus-arms dance move and put on a whiny voice. 'Full Force!'

That rocked him. He stepped back, clearly upset.

'Shut up!' he said, cracks in his voice. 'I'm gonna win that talent show, just you watch, and you're gonna wish you were up on stage with me!'

I felt a storm cloud in my stomach. Something dark brewing, and moving up into my throat, and I tried to stop myself. I swear I did, but I was too late, it just came out. I looked my oldest friend in the eye and said, 'The only thing you're winning is the biggest loser competition, idiot. You can't dance!'

Pause.

I will never forget the look on his face right then.

It was like someone had just taken out his batteries. His whole body seemed to slump. The noise of the supermarket fell quiet. Dom stumbled backwards a couple of steps, and then crumpled back into sitting on the floor.

And I felt awful.

If guilt has a colour, right then somebody dropped a dustbin full of it over me like paint.

I tried to speak, but I couldn't. I looked down at my oldest friend, battered by the meanness of the words that just came out of my big mouth.

38

The car journey home was like the quiet after an explosion. Mum was talking about the curry recipe, but I couldn't hear what she was saying. My ears, in fact my whole body, were still ringing with guilt, and there, underneath the ringing, two words, covered in spikes: **MR LIAR.**

When we got home, I ran straight upstairs and crashed on to my bed. **Mr Liar. Mr Liar.** The words were crawling over my skin like bugs. I felt rotten from the inside out. I don't know if you get travel sick on long car journeys or those baking-hot coach rides on school trips, but that's what I felt like. Like any second, I was going to puke.

I got up and opened my window, praying for fresh air to save me. Gus murmured something down by my feet. I looked at him, curled up like a

MR LIAR MR LIAR MR
Mr Liar
MR LIAR MR LIAR MR LIAR LIAR

horseshoe toilet brush. He looked so happy, I wished we could swap lives, just for a little while. He could be me in all this sick-feeling mess, and I could be him, peacefully snoozing under the radiator without a care in the world. **Mr Liar. Mr Liar.** I could hear the words on the breeze.

I sat down on the edge of my bed and looked at my wall. The map had so many of my scribbled words on it now, it was hard to even make out where the countries were.

Mr Liar.

I held my stomach and closed my eyes, trying to steady myself. **Mr Liar. Mr Liar.**

'Stop it!'

Gus lifted his head and looked at me. Into me. His warm, friendly eyes full of love.

'I'm not a liar, am I, Gus?'

Mr Liar.

I took a deep breath. 'You've known me all my life, right? Am I a liar?'

Gus tilted his head and . . .

OK, look. What I'm going to tell you now, I know how crazy it's going to sound. I don't expect you to believe me. There's a part of me that still doesn't even believe it myself. But it's what I remember, so I'm just going to tell you.

Gus tilted his head and, in his gruff, doggy voice, barked, 'Yep.'

There was a pause for maybe three seconds when the pair of us just sat staring at each other, then Gus curled back up and closed his eyes

And right then, the only thing I could manage to do was copy him. Still feeling sick, **Mr Liar** still crawling over my skin, I curled up on my bed, pulled my duvet up over my head, closed my eyes and tried to sleep.

Time is a funny thing, isn't it?

How many times have you checked the clock before bedtime and seen you had nearly an hour before you have to brush your teeth, then you blink and check the clock again and it says you only have five minutes?

Or, how many times have you been sitting in class in your last lesson of the day and the clock says five minutes left before the bell, so you get on with your work, happy that it's almost time to go home. Then when you check again, it still says five minutes?

What is that? Some evil game that clocks play on us? Is it the power of our own minds to project our fears and control time with some bad telekinetic juju?

I don't know. What I do know is, during that weekend, I stayed in bed feeling awful the whole time, and time seemed to disappear. It got dark at night and light in the day, but I had no idea what time it was at any point, and all I could hear were two little poisonous words.

Mr Liar.

Mum brought me dry toast and water when I told her I felt ill. But what I was feeling was something not even the greatest super-boss nurse could fix.

I'd done this to myself, and now I was stuck in it. Covered in lies.

So I just lay there, not asleep, but not really awake, and then I blinked and it was Monday morning.

Week Five

39

Sitting in my seat on Monday morning as Mr Bukowski took the register, I felt more out of place than I ever had in my life. If there was one word that would not be right to describe how I felt, it would be 'cool'. My eyes were stinging from lack of sleep. I felt hungry and queasy at the same time and those two words were still rattling round in the basement of my brain: **Mr Liar. Mr Liar.**

Everyone else was super-hyped. Last week of term. Last week of our primary school lives. On Friday we would break up for summer and say goodbye to this place, and everyone was pumped up about our big send-off: THE TALENT SHOW.

Mr Bukowski went round checking names of people who were going to perform, and double-checking what their acts would be

257

for the programme he was going to print out for the audience.

Andy Roberts was going to do magic tricks. Jamie Woon had trained his pet mouse to walk on a piece of string like a tightrope. Marcia Brown & Lucy Cheung were planning a full-on gymnastics routine to some famous pop song. As people talked, the whole room crackled with excitement.

Except for me.

I just sat in my seat, near the back, wishing I was at home, curled up under my radiator.

Then Dominic put his hand up.

'Sir!'

Mr Bukowski hushed the class. 'What is it, Dominic?'

'I need to change my act, sir.'

I felt my stomach turn over. Dominic hadn't even acknowledged me when I walked into class earlier. He just sat facing forward like I didn't exist.

'It's just a solo dance piece now, sir. Just me on my own.'

Mr Bukowski made notes. 'I see, and may I ask why that is?'

Dominic still had his hand up. 'My partner's not up to it, sir. He's all talk.'

'Oh, well, I'm sorry to hear that, Dom.'

Dom turned and looked right at me, his eyes like knives.

'Yes, sir. I'm sorry too.'

I felt like I was shrinking in my chair. And I wanted to. I wanted to just shrivel up and disappear. Nothing felt like it mattered. **Mr Liar.** Then the bell went for first break and everyone started packing up. I didn't move. My plan was to hang behind and avoid Dom, and everyone else. Just me on my own. **Mr Liar. Mr Liar.**

And then Danny Jones was standing right next to my table, smiling like a dog outside a butcher's window. Dad's letter. Monday morning. Our routine. I hadn't done it!

I'd spent the whole weekend in bed curled up, hiding from the world, and forgotten all about it. Now Danny Jones was standing right there, waiting for his new assignment to help Dad on the mission I'd made up at the start of it all.

'Silly me,' I said, slapping myself on the side of the head, trying to come up with an excuse. 'I've left it at home, Danny. Sorry.'

The look on Danny's face. Like that same dog outside the butcher's if you came out carrying steaks for yourself and offered him a bowl of Brussels sprouts. He was gutted. Getting the letter from Dad and a new research assignment was his favourite part of the week. For a moment, I genuinely thought he might burst into tears. I watched him compose himself and put on a brave face.

'That's all right,' he said. 'I'll come back to yours after school and get it then.'

I was so glad he didn't ask any more questions, I just agreed. I figured I could distract him with something when we got back and quickly scribble a fake letter from Dad. As I packed my bag, all I was thinking was, Thank God there's only one week of school left.

I spent the rest of the day hiding.

Lunchtime, I sat alone in a cubicle in the library toilets. I told myself if I didn't speak to anyone, if I didn't open my mouth, nothing else could come out.

A couple of times people came up to me asking about stories I'd made up in the weeks before. But each time they did, I just pretended I had to go and see a teacher or take a note to the school office and got away as soon as I could.

Dear Mr Liar,
Mr Liar. Mr Liar. Mr Liar.
Liar
   Liar
      Liar   Liar . . .

Walking home by myself, I felt like I was dragging a skip behind me. A massive metal bin, full of all the stuff I had made up since the start of term. All the things that had made me feel cool now felt like they belonged at the dump.

When Danny Jones caught up with me, out of breath, I'd completely forgotten he was coming back to ours.

'I waited for you,' he said, smiling. 'Where'd you go?'

'Sorry,' I said. 'Lot on my mind.'

'That's OK. I know the feeling.' He smiled again and we walked together. Me and my friend Danny Jones. I almost smiled. It seemed so weird now that I'd ever been scared of him.

40

When we got back to the house, nobody was home. Mum had already left for her shift, and Donna wouldn't be back until it was time to throw a pizza in the oven for me.

I took Danny to the kitchen and made us a Ribena.

'Are you OK?' he asked as we sipped, and I realized I was staring out of the window like Mum did.

'Yeah. Sorry. I just . . . Yeah.'

'You know, it's good to share problems, you know? My mum always says that.'

He smiled at me, and I felt alone, standing in my own kitchen.

'You ever feel like you've just made a big mess?' I said.

Danny put his empty glass on the side. 'Are

you kidding? All the time! I think it might be my superpower!'

He puffed up his chest and struck a Superman pose. And I laughed. Out loud. For what felt like the first time in absolutely ages.

'I need the toilet,' said Danny. 'Then let's read the letter.'

I'd forgotten all about the letter from Dad that I still had to fake. I pointed him upstairs, put our glasses in the sink, then, as he went out into the hall, I quickly ran through into the living room, grabbed a piece of paper and a pen from the shelves, sat down and started to fake the letter from Dad.

Where was he going this time? How many of these had I written now?

Mr Liar.

Shut up. I'm trying to concentrate.

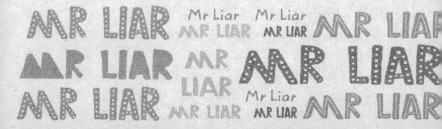

Mr Liar.

Shut up.

Alaska. Yeah. That's where he's going. Cold. Remote. Bears. Danny will love it.

I started to write.

Mr Liar.

Dear. **Mr Liar.** No.

Please stop it. But I couldn't. The only words I could hear were **Mr Liar.**

And then I realized where I was sitting.

In Dad's chair.

And the room started to spin. I gripped the arms to steady myself.

Dad's chair.

Dad.

Mr Liar.

I could see myself. Younger. Maybe five. Sitting on the floor in front of the chair. Donna

next to me. Both of us looking up at him. Waiting. For a magical story. From Dad.

I blinked and there I was. Five years old, looking up at Dad as he told a story. My whole body feeling full with the magic of it. The smile on his face. The fun.

I blinked again and I was back in the room. The piece of paper in my lap. Pen in my hand. Waiting for me to fake a letter from Dad. **Mr Liar.**

And it hit me in the back of the head, like Thor's hammer.

This wasn't magic. What I was doing wasn't fun at all. I felt awful. Dominic wouldn't speak to me. And the only words I could hear were **Mr Liar. Mr Liar. Mr Liar.**

No.

I'm not him.

'I'm not him!'

The words came out of my mouth like a burst of flame. And I meant them.

No more stories. No more fake letters. No more lies.

Right there and then, I decided to come clean. Starting with Danny Jones, right now.

If he got mad, so be it. If he went into a rage and knocked me out in my own living room, that's just the price I'd have to pay. I liked him. Maybe if I told him the truth – the real truth – maybe we could still be friends.

I was on my feet in a flash. I left the paper and pen and walked out into the hall.

'Danny!'

I started up the stairs.

'Danny! I need to tell you somethi—'

I stood there, at the top of the stairs.

The bathroom door was open, and it was empty.

My bedroom door was open too and, as I stepped forward, there was a sound.

A horrible sound.

Danny Jones was sitting on the edge of my bed. Crying.

And what was making him cry?

My wall.

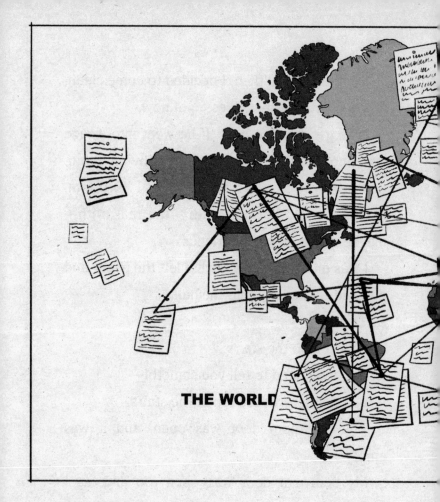

THE WORLD

The map.

Covered in everything I'd made up. The jagged pieces of all the stories I'd made up to try and be cool. What I'd said. Who I'd said it to. Danny's name plastered all over it. One big web of lies. I just stood there, frozen.

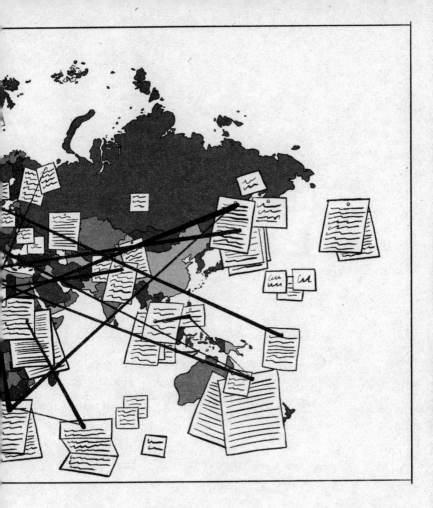

'Danny, I . . . I . . .'

Danny looked at me, through thick, real tears and said:

'It's all lies?'

And then he left.

41

What's the worst you've ever felt?

I mean, like, ever. The very worst?

There are different versions of feeling bad, right? Lots of different reasons and ways to feel like you just want someone to press DELETE on the playlist of your life, just so the feeling will go away.

If someone does something horrible or mean to you, that feels rubbish. You feel confused about why another human being could do something so mean. You close your eyes and just hope everything disappears because it's like the whole world is an unfair and nasty theme park that you wish your mum could come and pick you up from.

That's one way.

Here's my theory, though. There's a worse one.

And that's knowing that YOU are the person who has made someone else feel that bad.

Something you have said or done has made another human being want to curl up and disappear.

That's the worst.

That's when you have all the horrible feeling of the first kind, but on top of that is the guilty poison that runs through your blood from knowing that all of it is your own fault. You did that to someone. To more than one person.

And it feels like your skin is made of mistakes.

That's how I felt.

The rest of the week was horrible.

My oldest friend Dominic Clarke wouldn't speak to me. Now my newest friend Danny Jones couldn't even look me in the eye.

Sitting in class, each day that week, was like slow torture.

Everything felt like it was covered in what I

had done. My desk. The walls. The lunch hall. Playground. Home. Every single surface grafittied with my guilt.

There was nowhere to hide from it, and the worst part was, I knew I deserved it.

Danny Jones didn't tell anyone.

I never really understood that. Maybe he was just too angry, or upset.

Maybe he was embarrassed that I'd tricked him.

Maybe he was actually just too nice a guy underneath all that old hard-man persona from before. I'm not sure, but whatever the reason, a big part of me wished he had. I was pretty sure it wasn't possible for me to feel any worse, and maybe if he told people about my lies, everyone could have got angry and had a go at me, and then at least it would all be out in the open. Out of me. We were leaving junior school on Friday, so maybe I could just take all the abuse, then leave for the summer and try and start over. A clean slate, without the lies.

But he didn't.

So I had to sit in the guilty mess I'd made, for that whole week. People kept coming up to me asking about Dad, or wanting me to retell a particular story I'd made up over the last five weeks. Stories that had made me feel cool now all felt like rotten fruit sitting in my stomach.

I dodged everyone, made excuses, the whole time keeping my mouth shut, terrified of what might come out.

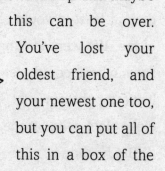

I made it through to Thursday afternoon. The last day but one of my junior school life.

Packing my bag at home time, I was telling myself: Just one more day. One more day and then we break up and maybe this can be over. You've lost your oldest friend, and your newest one too, but you can put all of this in a box of the

past and bury it somewhere, then try and get on with your life. A box with two words on the lid: **Mr Liar.**

As everyone else left the classroom, I thought I saw Dominic glance my way, just for a split second. But it was just wishful thinking. I'd hurt him too badly.

I hung back till everyone was gone, so that I wouldn't have to face any of them outside or on the way home. Then, just as I was stepping out of the room, I heard the calmest voice in the world.

'Jason? Can I have a word?'

42

I sat down in the same chair next to his desk.

Lazy rays of afternoon sun gave the whiteboard behind him a warm glow, like one of those background curtains they use for passport photographs.

Mr Bukowski leaned back in his chair, crossed one leg over the other, and smiled his friendly shaven-bear smile. I just wanted to go home, curl up in bed and block out the world.

'How are you?' he said, and I thought I was going to cry. The softness of his voice felt like a blanket I could hide under. My throat went tight, and I knew if I tried to speak, the tears would come, so I just offered half a nod.

'Is there anything you'd like to tell me?' he said. And that's when the feeling came.

Deep down inside me, like it was underneath

my stomach. The same crackle that started it all, but different. Stronger. Like the rumble before a volcano erupts deep under the sea. Mr Bukowski was staring at me and something in his eyes sparkled.

The crackle rose into my chest. Then up, into my throat. I felt my body sitting up straight in my chair. Mr Bukowski sat forward too, a look of excitement on his face. I thought I was going to burst. He grinned at me and nodded and I opened my mouth and . . .

It all came out.

Everything.

Dad. Mum. Donna. Not getting answers. The toothbrush. Questions. Frustration. The chain reaction. The mission. Danny Jones. Dominic. The stories. Wanting to be cool. My wall. The map. Not sleeping. The guilt. How sorry I was. How rotten I felt. How I wished it had never started. How I knew how mean I'd been. How I just wanted to go back in time and put everything right. Make things good with

Dom. With Danny. With everyone.

All of it rushed out of my mouth like a rainbow of truth and as it did, it felt **INCREDIBLE.**

When I finally finished, and slumped back into my chair, I felt like I'd just climbed out from under an avalanche. Like I could breathe again. Like I was clean.

I sat there, breathing what felt like new air, and waited for Mr Bukowski to tell me off. To explain what I already knew. How I'd messed up. How I deserved everything that had happened.

But he didn't.

He just sat there. Smiling. And then he said something I will never forget. He said:

'It's a bit like a fireman's hose.'

I didn't understand.

'Sir?'

Mr Bukowski gestured with his hands. 'A fireman's hose. If you don't know where to point it. It gets messy.'

I didn't know where to look. And my face must've been a muddle of confusion, because he leaned even further forward and said, 'What I mean, young man, is that I think we've found your talent.'

Then the pair of us sat in the empty classroom for nearly an hour, and he told me what he thought I should do.

43

Are you scared of spiders?

Snakes?

Sharks?

Cheese? The stinky ones with the blue veins in?

Old people's feet?

Tell the truth.

Me too. Gross, right?

See, there's different types of scared though, right?

There's the type of scared that will turn a regular normal coat, hanging up in your wardrobe, into a werewolf when you turn your bedroom light off.

There's the type of scared that turns your stomach inside out when you're standing on the edge of the highest diving board at the swimming pool.

There's the type of scared that will make your tongue stop working when there's somebody that you really like and you can't tell them.

Then there's the type of scared you feel when you know there's something that you have to do, but you don't know what's going to happen when you do it.

And that's the type of scared I felt as I sat in the packed lunch hall that Friday morning. Last day of term.

TALENT SHOW

It was rammed.

All the students. All the teachers. A big handful of parents. Dinner ladies. Even a bunch of Year 7s from Wakens Tip High school, for some reason. All crammed in to watch the acts perform. And I

282

sat in the middle of the front row, with my plan, my stomach like a ticking time bomb.

One by one, people got up and did their thing.

Andy Roberts did his magic tricks. They were all right (you could kind of see the flowers up his sleeve).

Two girls from Year 4 sang a Disney song standing on stilts.

Jamie Woon's mouse got stage fright and fainted.

Marcia Brown & Lucy Cheung did a full-on gymnastics routine to that song 'Danger Zone' wearing matching sparkling leotards and ribbons and everything. It was pretty amazing. At the end they shot purple glitter from cannons out over the audience and everyone went crazy.

Except me.

I just sat there, purple glitter raining down all around me, knowing it was almost my time.

There was only one act left to go. One more act that had to follow the best, most spectacular and most glittery gymnastic routine ever.

Dominic Clarke. Waiting on the end of the front row for his turn.

As the glitter settled and quiet fell across the audience, I seized my moment.

I jumped out of my seat, climbed up on to the stage and tapped the microphone.

'Hell— erm . . . Hello?'

A sea of faces stared up at me. I could feel my own pulse throbbing in my skin. This was it. Come on, Jay. Stick to the plan.

'Hello. Everyone. There's something I have to say.'

I scanned the confused faces, looking for someone. Someone important.

Danny Jones was sitting halfway back on the right. I looked right at him. This boy that I'd hurt. That I'd lied to. My friend.

See, sometimes the best thing to say is exactly what you mean, and nothing else.

I took a deep breath.

'I'm sorry.'

There was the murmur from the crowd. I kept

my eyes on Danny. He stared back at me. I thought of everything that I wanted to tell him. All the things I wanted to say.

'I'm sorry.'

Danny just stared.

I forced myself not even to blink as I stared back.

Then he smiled. Danny Jones smiled.

I smiled back.

People in the audience were looking at each other now, like, 'Why is he apologizing to us?' But it didn't matter. This was the plan, and it wasn't over.

I looked across at Mr Bukowski, who was standing next to the stage behind the curtain, triggering music for the acts. He smiled a friendly shaven-bear smile and nodded.

Then I looked down at Dominic, sitting on the end of the first row, looking more confused than anyone. I stared right at him. My oldest friend. I took another deep breath.

'I'm so sorry.'

Everything seemed to freeze, as I hung there

in hope, waiting for him to respond. Please. Please. *Please*.

Then Dom smiled.

That perfect crooked smile I hadn't seen for weeks. The smile that mattered the most. And right then, it felt like lightning kissed my heart.

But I wasn't done. There was one more thing left to do.

I gestured to Dom to come up on stage with me. As he climbed up, I looked at Mr Bukowski and nodded. He gave me a thumbs up and pressed PLAY.

There was crackle through the speakers.

'I'm sorry, everyone . . . but what you're about to see . . . just might blow your mind.'

I glanced at Dom, now standing next to me as the horns from James Brown's 'Cold Sweat (Part One)' blasted out full volume. I grabbed the microphone and puffed up my chest.

'Ladies and gentlemen! Boys and girls! And teachers! Prepared to be smacked in the face, and ears, by the power of . . . FULL FORCE!'

Dominic nudged me. 'Yo. What do we do?'

I grinned my biggest grin. 'We dance!' I punched the air. 'Full Foooooorce!'

Then me and best friend, closed our eyes, and did . . .

the . . .

worst . . .

dance . . .

routine . . .

EVER . . .

SEEN.

And embarrassed ourselves more than anyone ever has since schools were first invented – and became school legends.

44

And that is how my junior school life ended.

That is how I won back the trust of my oldest friend.

And how I made a new one in Danny Jones.

And how I learned the true meaning of the word 'cool'.

To me, real cool isn't getting the most attention, or being the most popular.

REAL cool is doing the things you love to do, with the people who matter the most.

A lot happened in those few weeks. Enough to almost fill a book. And you'd think that would be that, wouldn't you?

But that's the funny thing about stories.

Sometimes, what you think is the end is actually just the beginning.

Later that evening, after dinner, as me and Donna cleared the plates from the table, Mum stood with her glass of wine looking out of the living-room window.

Word had somehow spread to Wakens Tip High School about Full Force's insanely bad talent-show debut, and Donna was asking for details, in between giggling.

'So your eyes were closed the whole time?'

I laughed along with her. 'Yep. Then, when the song finished and I opened them . . . Well, have you ever seen a couple of hundred people dumbstruck?'

She started filling up the sink. 'I can't say that I have. How did it feel?'

My whole body was glowing as I remembered Dominic's face. 'It felt awesome.'

'Holy French toast!' Mum shouted from the living room. 'Come and look at this!'

There was a crowd of people on Mr Benn's lawn next door. One man in a brown jacket was on his knees holding an expensive camera, and there, standing on his front doorstep, in between two grinning women in purple bathing suits, was Mr Benn, holding a giant cheque.

I felt my jaw drop open.

'I think he's won the lottery,' said Mum.

'That says two-point-three million!' said Donna, her eyes wide as headlights.

I looked at Mr Benn. At the photographer. Then at Mum, and Donna.

I didn't say anything, but I knew that I'd thought it up, imagined it, the scene on Mr Benn's lawn right now, before it happened. I knew that much. What did it mean? I didn't know.

What I knew was, primary school was finished. A big chunk of my life done. And in front of me lay a long summer, and then a whole new life at secondary school. I had absolutely no idea what was coming, but I felt a crackle . . .

deep down in my stomach . . .

starting . . .

to . . .

move.

ABOUT THE AUTHOR

Steven Camden is one of the UK's most acclaimed spoken word artists. He writes for stage, page and screen, teaches storytelling and leads creative projects all over the place.

He has performed his work all around the world from Manchester to Melbourne and Kuala Lumpur to California. He moved to London for a girl, but Birmingham is where he's from.

He also has a thing for polar bears.

In 2019, his first poetry collection for children, *Everything All at Once*, won the CLiPPA award.

ABOUT THE ILLUSTRATOR

Chanté Timothy is an illustrator who creates work that often explores different themes of diversity. She loves experimenting with movement, expression and storytelling through her characters.

Chanté's first book debut called *A Black Woman Did That* by Malaika Adero in 2020 helped kick-start her passion for children's book illustration.

Drawing for as long as she can remember, she'd always been that strange kid who'd ask for paper and pen to entertain herself instead of playing with dolls.

SUMMER SCHOOL AND CYBORGS

STEVEN CAMDEN

Coming in summer 2022

School. Heaven, hell, waiting for the bell.

EVERY-
THING
ALL AT ONCE

STEVEN
AKA POLARBEAR
CAMDEN

CLPPA
WINNER 2019

'He's just brilliant' Kae Tempest
'His craft is unique' Scroobius Pip